Kavan
TWENTY-FIVE years
(1972–1997)

Ravan
TWENTY-FIVE years (1972–1997)

A commemorative volume of new writing

Edited by G E de Villiers

RAVAN PRESS

Published by Ravan Press, 1997
PO Box 145 Randburg 2125 South Africa

Each contribution copyright © the author.

All rights reserved. No part of this publication may be
reproduced, stored in a retrieval system, or transmitted in any
form or by any means, electronic, mechanical, photocopying,
or otherwise, without the prior permission of the copyright
owner.

Cover design: Centre Court Studio
Typesetting: Niamb Simons

ISBN 0 86975 496 3

Printed in South Africa by Creda Press (Pty) Ltd, Eliot Avenue, Eppindust II

Contents

Introduction

PART 1
The Background

The Beginnings of Ravan Press: a memoir	Peter Randall	1
Ringing the changes – Twenty-five years of Ravan Press	Glenn Moss	13
Publishing the Past: Ravan Press and Historical Writing	Albert Grundlingh	24

PART 2
New Writing

Boyhood	JM Coetzee	35
Four Poems	Chris van Wyk	41
Athol Fugard and the New South Africa	Mary Benson	50
Pulled In	Yvonne Burgess	56
St Francis in the Veld	Christopher Hope	66
The Man Who Had Everything – A Fable	Peter Wilhelm	76
The Banquet	Ahmed Essop	85
A True Romance	Stephen Gray	93
Three Poems	Ingrid de Kok	103
Martha, Martha What's Your Boy's Name?	Mongane Wally Serote	107
A Gem Squash	Rose Moss	116
Enemy	Lionel Abrahams	134
Silences (a poem)	Es'kia Mphahlele	143
Look-alikes	Nadine Gordimer	150

Acknowledgements 159

Introduction

November 1997 marks the 25th anniversary of Ravan Press. The purpose of this volume is to commemorate the occasion.

It is, I think, generally conceded that much of the history of Ravan Press is inextricably bound up with the struggle against apartheid. From the outset, it registered its opposition to racial discrimination and the political ideology underpinning it. A voice was given to the oppressed and their cause championed. Publications, usually radical in character, became the chief weapons in the onslaught against social injustice. Some of these attracted the unwelcome attention of the state. Retaliation was inevitable and frequently took the form of intimidatory action. An added aggravation was the not infrequent headache of financial insecurity. Yet, in spite of the problems (and various fluctuations in fortune) Ravan Press has managed to survive, even if barely at times!

Elsewhere in these pages Peter Randall, a founding member of Ravan and still active in its affairs, recounts his involvement with the "bird" from conception up to 1977. After briefly revisiting some of the ground covered by Randall, the immediate past Managing Director, Glenn Moss, takes over the reins and continues with the story up to recent times.

I am particularly sorry about the absence of a retrospective from Mike Kirkwood. His incumbency spanned the years between Randall and Moss. Regrettably, I was not able to make contact with him. This is a great pity, for a personal account of his Ravan years — some of which were particularly turbulent — would have been of considerable interest. Fortunately, however, Glenn Moss, during the course of his article, highlights both the period, and the value of Kirkwood's contribution to it.

Randall, Kirkwood and Moss, successively at the helm of Ravan, constituted a formidable trio. Supported by a committed staff, none ever flinched from publishing what he considered to be necessary and worthwhile, no matter if this resulted in stern opposition, unwarranted harassment, or even the threat of bodily harm. What they left behind was a legacy of some of the best work produced in this country. They also attracted a notable array of authors.

This was brought to mind in an exercise conducted by the *Mail & Guardian*, a Johannesburg weekly newspaper. It decided to canvass a range of informed opinions in an attempt to establish which were "the 10 best South African novels of the past ten years". An impossible task, of course! The result (published in the August 15 to 21 1997 edition) was, if nothing else, interesting. Of the ten novels chosen, five were written by authors who had, at one time or another, been published by Ravan. They were Stephen Gray, JM Coetzee, Nadine Gordimer, Zakes Mda and Chris van Wyk. To these should be added the names of Christopher Hope and Peter Wilhelm, who were mentioned more than once in the survey but without quite reaching the top ten. With the exception of Zakes Mda, the rest of the writers are represented in this volume, mostly by works not previously published.

I don't think I'm wrong in saying that much of Ravan's publishing has been determined by quality rather than category. Over the years it has therefore served as a vehicle for all forms of (good) writing. Most prominent among these are, perhaps, what might loosely be termed works of history, and works of the imagination. Because much of this volume is engaged with the more "creative" side, it was decided, as a kind of counterbalance, to include an assessment of Ravan's contribution to the historical debate. In this regard I am indebted to Professor Albert Grundlingh for his article entitled *Publishing the Past: Ravan Press and Historical Writing*. In this fascinating overview he confidently tackles the daunting task of attempting to quantify the "impact of Ravan's historical publications" – and succeeds admirably in achieving the aim. A further dimension is added by his personal recollections of Ravan during the "struggle years".

When the idea of a commemorative volume was first mooted, it was decided to invite contributions, mainly of a literary kind, from past and present Ravan authors, but without being prescriptive about genre or subject matter. What we expected was a range of topics. This did not materialize. Instead, a surprising number of contributions were informed by a single focus and a similarity of theme.

To start with, a cluster of writers opted to set their material in the period after the 1994 election. It is not surprising, then, to encounter the commonality of phrases such as: "new South African factors" (Stephen Gray); "shortly after the election" (Peter Wilhelm); "the new South Africa" (Mary Benson); "after the Apartheid era" (Ahmed Essop); "now that apartheid's over" (Rose Moss), and so on. To this should be added *Transfer* (that is, from the old to the new) and *At the commission*, the titles of two poems by Ingrid de Kok.

Then, in quite a few of the stories and poems, there is a sense that historical change has only been partially achieved; that the "new South Africa" has not yet totally succeeded in unshackling itself from the past; and, consequently, that the act of transformation still has some way to go.

Although used in a different context, these words from Stephen Gray's *A True Romance* epitomize the attitude: "... the kind of social barriers for which South Africa is famous" still has the effect of keeping us "from settling down", notwithstanding the fact that the transition from "apartheid to democracy had occurred smoothly enough".

In not dissimilar vein is the interplay between two characters in Mongane Wally Serote's *Martha, Martha What's Your Boy's Name?*: the one says that "the struggle has brought many people together", to which the other replies, "there is still something which makes us different".

Lionel Abrahams is more sanguine. In the story entitled *Enemy*, a chance encounter reunites a bully with an erstwhile victim. Feared and hated in the past, the bully looks less than ordinary in the present.

It is perhaps, for this reason, that the "victim", who had expected to feel bitter, is instead suffused with a "broadminded and worldly forgiveness" of, and a "feeling of brotherliness" towards, his former tormentor. The moment is intensely cathartic. Of course, the wider implications of the story need no elaboration.

In the last stanza of his poem *Silences* (August 1992–1993) Es'kia Mphahlele warns against the treachery of remaining silent while others

> "... betray for power
> or for money
> or for blood lust"

and is filled with sorrow when, while the country smoulders,

> "... presidents and premiers
> and entourage of sycophants
> wave their flags from limousines and luxury trains
> to assemble voting cattle".

That was how it was, but implicit in these words is the plea that the present (and the future) should never again be allowed to look like the past.

Although it predates almost all else in this volume (having first been published in a journal in 1992) the title – and import – of Nadine Gordimer's *Look-alikes*, is to me the perfect summation of much that appears in these pages. For this reason it seemed appropriate to round off the collection with this story.

Not everyone chose to write about the "past in the present". There is the deeply moving extract from JM Coetzee's autobiographical *Boyhood* (Secker & Warburg, 1997); the intensely felt poetic portraits of members of his family (Mother, Father, Auntie, Granny) by Chris van Wyk; the first chapter of Yvonne Burgess's new novel (a sequel to *Anna and the Colonel*, Ravan Press, 1997); and Christopher Hope's *St Francis in the Veld*, which is quite brilliant in its quirkiness.

Subtle, multifaceted, and beautifully crafted, every piece in this volume deserves to be savoured, but above all, to be read with enjoyment, for all are eminently readable.

It has become customary to conclude a book of this kind with a brief biographical sketch of each writer. I have decided to dispense with this, as the contributors are so well known that no introduction seemed necessary.

Perhaps just a word about where Ravan Press is today and my involvement in it. For more than a decade the company I work for (Hodder & Stoughton) has been co-publishing works, mainly children's stories, with Ravan Press. In 1994 we acquired a majority shareholding in Ravan; the balance of the shares remain with the Ravan Trust, which currently consists of five members.

At the end of his article, Albert Grundlingh ponders on the "future direction of Ravan". Given the depressed state of the book trade (both nationally and internationally) I suppose the only satisfactory answer is that time alone – and possibly the demands of readers, both on a cultural and scholarly level – will tell.

Finally, my grateful thanks to our distinguished panel of authors for their contributions. Their presence in this book is the best tribute that can be paid to Ravan Press in celebration of its 25 years of existence.

GE de Villiers
Ravan Press

PART 1

The Background

Peter Randall
The Beginnings of Ravan Press: a memoir

In a letter to me, Lionel Abrahams generously wrote that Ravan Press has had "a unique and tremendously significant history". The significance of Ravan's history, of its contribution to South Africa's cultural and political life, must be judged on the basis of the several hundred titles and the important new writers that it has published over the past quarter century.

As the only person who has had an unbroken association with Ravan throughout its life, variously as director, publisher, editor, trustee and consultant, perhaps I can say something about its early history. That history is, indeed, unique among South African publishing houses.

I shall concentrate on Ravan's beginnings and early years, until October 1977. In that month I was banned for five years by the South African government under the Internal Security Act and was no longer able, at least officially, to carry on working for Ravan. Although I continued, clandestinely, to read and edit manuscripts and to meet with the new directors for policy discussions, my involvement was necessarily reduced. New directors, notably Mike Kirkwood, Glenn Moss and Gerald de Villiers, led Ravan through its subsequent history. I hope they will write about their years with Ravan.

My own account is by no means comprehensive and exhaustive. It is merely a personal reminiscence, following a simple chronological structure, in which I try to record the major milestones in Ravan's first few years. The context, of course, was one of severe repression by the state of any activity, including publishing, that was regarded as being inimical to its interests. Much of that repression was quite arbitrary and relatively junior officials of the security apparatus had considerable power to act against those who opposed state policies. The Congress movement having been outlawed in the 1960s, the state regarded Black Consciousness as one of its prime internal targets in the early 1970s, and any manifestations of it were dealt with with varying degrees of severity. This included not only organizations like the Black People's Convention and individuals like Steve Biko, but also the written, even the spoken, word.

It is thus not surprising that very few established local publishing houses dared to publish any but the most innocuous writings of both black and white South Africans. But the silence of the sixties that Nadine Gordimer has written about in *The Black Interpreters* was giving way in the early seventies to a wave of protest writing, especially in verse, and a group of small, independent publishers was emerging who dared to publish some of this output. Ravan Press, David Philip and Ad Donker came into existence at roughly the same historical moment, quite independently of each other. Whereas the latter two were commercial ventures, aiming to produce honest profits, Ravan was born out of an intense idealism that, now, may seem somewhat quaint and in which the profit motive did not feature at all.

To understand this idealism, and to understand Ravan's early history, one must go back to Spro-cas (the Study Project on Christianity in Apartheid Society). This study project was sponsored by the Christian Institute and the South African Council of Churches from 1969 to 1972 to explore and present alternatives to apartheid. To this end, six study commissions were set up in the fields of politics, education, the church, law, the economy and social relationships. The commissions were composed of academics, writers, clergy, trade unionists, businessmen and politicians, many of whom have had distinguished public careers.

As the director of Spro-cas, it was my task to co-ordinate the work of the different commissions and to see to the publication of their final reports. These reports were preceded by a series of occasional publications in which some of the more significant working papers and contributions by individual commissioners were made available. These occasional publications bore such titles as *Anatomy of Apartheid*, *Directions of Change in South Africa*, and *Some Implications of Inequality*. The Spro-cas commission reports themselves appeared between 1970 and 1972: they included *Education beyond Apartheid*, *Power, Privilege and Poverty*, and *South Africa's Political Alternatives*, and were followed by *A Taste of Power*, the final Spro-cas report, which I wrote and which paid considerable attention to Black Consciousness as well as to the sins of the government.

The study project was followed by Spro-cas 2, a project for social change. It, too, published material relating to South African affairs and, particularly, the need for radical change in the country's policies. This material ranged from provocative posters intended to arouse white consciences to serious studies of national issues like migrant labour. There are three things in particular about Spro-cas which are relevant to the beginnings of Ravan Press.

In the first place, Spro-cas 2 was structured into a Black Community Programme (BCP) run by Bennie Khoapa and Steve Biko, and a social change programme aimed primarily at whites and directed by former student activists such as Neville Curtis and Horst Kleinschmidt. Under the aegis of Spro-cas, the BCP launched a publishing programme which included *Black Review*, intended as an annual survey of the nation's life from a black perspective, and *Black Viewpoint*, a collection of essays by such writers as Biko himself and Njabulo Ndebele. Here was the potential genesis of an independent, indigenous black publishing house, but it did not survive the banning of Biko and his subsequent death at the hands of the security police, and the banning of the BCP itself in 1977. But what had been clearly demonstrated was that there was both a need and a demand for the kind of radical black writing that the BCP had produced.

Secondly, Spro-cas was intended as a relatively short-term venture and, as it came to its end in 1973, it had put together a fairly substantial body of publications. These included, not only the BCP publications and the Spro-cas reports, but also several other titles which had been published with a view to contributing to the search for social justice in South Africa. These ranged from Rick Turner's essay on participatory democracy, *The Eye of the Needle*, to *Cry Rage*, a volume of protest poetry by James Matthews and Gladys Thomas which was introduced by Nadine Gordimer at a Spro-cas poetry evening in December 1972. *Cry Rage* evoked an enormous reaction. Stephen Gray called it "one big sobby tear", but most commentators recognized the genuine anger and hurt that the verse conveyed. Perhaps because the watchdogs were caught napping during the Christmas season, *Cry Rage* was not banned until March 1973, as it was about to be reprinted. In South African terms it had been a best-seller and several foreign language editions had been issued. The banning – the first of a volume of poems – raised a public outcry. Students and staff at Wits University, led by Jonathan Paton, held a meeting where they deliberately read from the book. The banning represented a considerable loss of funds to Spro-cas, as well as the loss of potential future income from sales. *The Eye of the Needle* was not itself banned, but the banning of its author effectively ended its distribution in this country. All these developments were portents of things to come for the yet to be established Ravan.

Altogether, Spro-cas published some 25 titles in what *International Affairs* described as "its short but amazingly productive history". With the termination of Spro-cas, it was necessary to establish a vehicle for the continued distribution of these titles, as well as to cope with the demand for new ones. By this time, many writers were viewing Spro-cas as a publisher in its own right and were submitting manuscripts for consideration. This situation was one of the factors that led to the decision to establish Ravan Press.

Thirdly, from the beginning, Spro-cas publications were produced in-house as it were, using the facilities of the Christian Institute, in particular an old Heidelberg offset machine bought with funds donated by German churches. The design, layout, paste-up, origination, printing, collating and binding were under the control of the brilliant Danie van Zyl, who transferred from the Christian Institute to Spro-cas and then to Ravan. Assisted by Isobel Randall, Van Zyl produced a series of eye-catching covers that helped to persuade even nervous booksellers to carry some of the Spro-cas titles. When Ravan Press (Pty) Ltd was established in the second half of 1972, its initial function was to act as a printer for Spro-cas and Christian Institute publications. As the Articles of Association made clear, however, the company was also intended in due course to publish in its own right. The decision to form a (Pty) Ltd company was taken on legal advice, largely because it was felt to be most unlikely that permission would be granted for the venture to be registered as a non-profit, charitable organization.

The founding directors and shareholders of Ravan were Beyers Naudé, director of the Christian Institute and the prime mover in establishing and obtaining funds for Spro-cas, the Rev. Danie van Zyl, and myself. The name was suggested by Van Zyl: Ra from Randall, va from Van Zyl, and n from Naudé. The name stuck, and has been regularly confused with the raven, a problem not helped by the bird emblem that was designed for us by Penguin's expert. Three shares of R1 were issued, one for each shareholder. The intention was that shares were to be held in trust, as it were, and that no financial benefit should accrue to shareholders. Thus, when Naudé and Van Zyl later withdrew as shareholders, both their shares were transferred to me with no monetary consideration, and when I was banned I simply handed over my shares to my successor and, again, no money changed hands. This was the position until his shareholding became something of a bargaining counter in Mike Kirkwood's divorce arrangements in the 1980s. At the same time, Kirkwood agreed to "donate" the bulk of his shareholding to the newly-established Ravan Trust.

At the time of Ravan's establishment, I was still preoccupied with completing my tasks in Spro-cas as well as acting as director of the short-lived Programme for Social Change (PSC), another outcome of Spro-cas in which Kleinschmidt played the major role until his detention and subsequent flight from the country. (One of the more bizarre encounters during the life of the PSC was a supposedly secret roof-top meeting with Breyten Breytenbach, which was carefully filmed by the security police. At Breytenbach's urging, the widow of Franz Fanon also visited the offices for another "secret" meeting. Since I could not believe that her movements were not being meticulously monitored, nothing much came of that.)

My own entanglement with the guardians of the state also left me with little opportunity to be actively involved in the affairs of the new press at first, and with Naudé busy in many directions, Danie van Zyl was the mainstay of Ravan's first months. He saw to the remaining printing needs of Spro-cas and secured contracts with other bodies, including NUSAS (National Union of South African Students). Ravan began life with two material assets: the printing and related equipment inherited from the Christian Institute, and the stock of Spro-cas publications. It was agreed that there would be no solicitation of foreign, or local, donations or grants and that Ravan was to be self-sufficient, surviving through its own efforts or not at all. This policy was maintained until after my banning in 1977, whereafter donations and grants were actively sought and were forthcoming, mainly from German church sources.

By the end of its first year, Ravan was clearly moving into the publishing gap left by the termination of Spro-cas. Its first titles were joint Ravan-Spro-cas publications, notably three "black" books published late in 1973 and early 1974: Gordimer's *The Black Interpreters*, *Black Nationalism in South Africa* by Peter Walshe, and *Being-black-in-the-world* by NC Manganyi. The first Ravan title to receive widespread press coverage was another book of poems, Wopko Jensma's *Sing for our Executive* (published jointly with Ophir, June 1973, at R2,50, and owing much to the enthusiasm of Walter Saunders).

Most serious commentators recognized Jensma's worth. Stephen Gray identified him as a major force in South African poetry and Peter Wilhelm said that his work was touched by genius. Even the Afrikaans press, which had steadfastly ignored most Spro-cas and Ravan titles, paid attention to this new book, not quite sure whether to claim Jensma as an Afrikaner or not. No doubt reflecting our obsession with race, many reviewers speculated on Jensma's identity. The indefatigable reviewer for the *Sunday Times*, the late Mary Morison Webster, was fairly certain that he was black, but not too sure where he came from:

> The reader's initial and, indeed, lasting impression is that Jensma is an African – possibly of Sophiatown. His use of words and phrases nevertheless seems, at times, that of an American negro rather than of a man of the Transvaal.

The security police were understandably rather confused by the links between Ravan, Spro-cas, the Programme for Social Change and the Christian Institute (a confusion compounded by the fact that I stood as a Social Democratic candidate in the 1974 general election), and tended to see all these as merely the different heads of the same godless, leftist monster. My first direct encounter with the security police had come in July 1972 with the confiscation of my passport, which was not finally returned to me, free of restrictions, for more than ten years. But, from the beginning, Ravan was plagued by the upholders of law and order.

In September 1973, the offices were raided three times in one week by plainclothes police looking for evidence to support a charge under the Suppression of Communism Act that Ravan had published the utterances of a banned person. This was Paul Pretorius, the president of NUSAS, whose words had appeared in a dossier published by Spro-cas on behalf of NUSAS and printed by Ravan. The dossier had already been printed when Pretorius was banned, and we had pasted a sheet of paper over the offending words. This sheet contained a message concocted by me which said much the same as Pretorius had. In what became known internally as the Great Prittstick Case, the directors of Ravan were duly summonsed and appeared in the Johannesburg Magistrate's Court (a warrant for my arrest had to be issued since I was unable to be present, as I was standing trial in Pretoria on the same day on a charge under the Commissions Act).

When the trial finally got under way our advocate, Johan

Kriegler, was able to convince the court that the police had charged the wrong people: Ravan was merely the printer and the real culprit presumably would have been the publishers, i.e. Spro-cas. Since, in the minds of the security branch, these were indistinguishable, their irritation was understandable.

In January 1974 they tried again, this time investigating a charge under the Publications and Entertainments Act for four posters which Ravan had published on behalf of Spro-cas. One carried a quotation from Adolf Hitler, another portrayed the "South African Education Machine" and two depicted "affluent whites dominating miserable blacks". I was quoted in the *Rand Daily Mail* at the time as saying that if the apartheid state charged us under the Act with harming race relations it would be a grotesque irony. In the event, no prosecution followed, but the waste of time and funds was, of course, enormously harmful to Ravan. The Great Prittstick Case actually dragged on until August 1974, and the state then appealed to the Supreme Court. The appeal was heard in September 1975 and in December it was rejected. Ravan was represented by Kriegler and Denys Williams, both of whom were later to become distinguished judges themselves.

In April 1974 it was mutually agreed that Ravan would cease to be a printing company, producing material for the Christian Institute. It would henceforth concentrate on publishing, with two main objectives: the continued distribution of Spro-cas and earlier Ravan publications, and the publication of new work in its own right. From the beginning the policy was to publish only material relating to contemporary southern African issues and to foster the work of new black writers. Merit was to be a major criterion in the selection of both literary and socio-political manuscripts.

Ravan's involvement in printing and the acquisition of printing equipment had caused the company severe financial strain, added to the costs involved in court cases. The Christian Institute was owed R51 000, then a substantial sum. It was agreed that the Institute would take over all the printing equipment, and launch a new printing company, Zenith Printers. Ravan would divest itself of any printing functions and would favour Zenith for its own printing requirements. Danie van Zyl moved to Tarkastad to be the Presbyterian minister there, and relinquished his directorship and shareholding in Ravan. I moved into a full-time role as director and publisher of Ravan, and indeed as editor and salesman.

In May 1974, Ravan published JM Coetzee's *Dusklands* to immediate critical acclaim. When Coetzee submitted *In the Heart of the Country* for the Mofolo-Plomer Prize which Ravan administered on behalf of the donors (Nadine Gordimer, Ad Donker, Bateleur Press and Ravan itself), I had no hesitation in writing to the author to say we would like to publish it. After some time Coetzee replied that a major British publisher was interested. Although our contract with him contained the usual clause about being offered his next work, I decided we could not stand in the way of possible international recognition and world sales and so the clause was not enforced. Coetzee negotiated with his new publisher to give Ravan South African rights and this was the position for several of his subsequent titles. It was painful to know that as a small publisher we could not compete with international houses to retain authors for whom we had taken the initial risks.

In 1974-1975 Ravan published several other literary firsts. These included *The World of Nat Nakasa*; Stephen Gray's first novel, *Local Colour*; Peter Wilhelm's collection of short stories, *LM and other stories*, which revealed an exciting new talent; Peter Horn's first volume of verse; and Miriam Tladi's *Muriel at Metropolitan*, a semi-autobiographical account of a black woman working in Johannesburg's commercial jungle. Tladi's manuscript consisted of a large ring binder crammed with disjointed writings including verses and prayers. It was clear, however, that embedded in this mass of material was an interesting and original narrative. Sheila Roberts was commissioned to edit the work and did so brilliantly, shaping it into a lean and publishable text while retaining the writer's own voice. The book launched Tladi on a writing career: Ravan subsequently published her *Amandla*, and it was disappointing when she later attacked the press on racial grounds and accused it of manipulating her work.

The trials of Christian Institute and Spro-cas staff under the Commissions Act, for refusing to testify before a secret parliamentary commission that was clearly a cover for punitive action without benefit of fair trial, were meanwhile dragging on. The trial of Beyers Naudé inevitably attracted much public attention: my own appearance was low-key in comparison, starting in May 1975 and concluding only in November 1976 with a two-month suspended sentence. The outcome was reasonably satisfactory, and the Schlebusch (later Le Grange) Commission was thoroughly discredited, contributing to the eventual collapse of the United Party which had collaborated with the government in the work of the commission. But, once again, although our legal costs were met by well-wishers, the loss of time and money – numerous journeys had to be undertaken to the court in Pretoria over a period of nearly three years – had its effect on the work of Ravan.

Nevertheless, at the end of its third year of operation, in August 1975, it was possible to report that Ravan had broken even, purely on its sales income which was running at about R3 000 a month. The accumulated deficit of R60 000 was also being steadily whittled away. The figures may seem derisory now: Ravan's running costs (including rent, telephone, stationery, salaries, etc) were then about R1 000 a month, and the annual budget, which included production, distribution and advertising expenses, was R35 000. At the same time thousands of rands were being lost through bannings. Jensma's second volume of poems and woodcuts, *Where White is the Colour, Where Black is the Number*, was gazetted within six months, the fourth Ravan title to be banned outright in just over two years. Bannings of individuals also caused heavy losses, as books had to be withdrawn or manually mutilated to remove offending passages.

In March 1976 we had the bizarre experience of appealing to the Publications Appeal Board against the banning of *Confused Mhlaba*, an innocuous and amusing little play by Mqayisa Khayalethu, which a publications committee had decided put the police in a bad light and was harmful to race relations. Despite our impressive array of expert witnesses who included Dr NC Manganyi, Dr Ampie Coetzee and Peter Wilhelm, the grey gentlemen of the Board decided the ban should stay. Such actions are, of course, self-defeating: *Index on Censorship* and Stephen Spender took up the matter and I wrote an article on the banning of *Confused Mhlaba* for them, several foreign language editions were published, some township performances were held on the grounds that the text had been banned but not the play itself, admittedly a delicate distinction, and the play enjoyed more attention than it might otherwise have done.

Although Ravan's image then was of a radical, risk-taking publisher prepared to test the limits of the apartheid state's tolerance, it was inevitable that some self-censorship had to be practised for sheer survival. One example I particularly regret was the decision to exclude a Peter-Dirk Uys play from *Contemporary South African Plays*, edited by the late Ernest Pereira and published in June 1976 (the play itself was in fact later banned). The company constantly walked a financial tightrope and further bannings could have been disastrous. Some bookshops were afraid to stock our titles and some were visited by the special branch to dissuade them from doing so. Our own operations were probably as lean as they could be. By the end of 1976 the staff consisted of myself, Patricia Kirkman as secretary-bookkeeper, and a messenger-cum-packer. My salary of around R300 a month was hardly adequate to maintain a young family.

The net also seemed to be closing during that period. Jimmy Kruger, the Minister of Justice, declared that certain whites were behind the emergence of Black Consciousness (presumably in the belief that blacks themselves were incapable of any such thing) and warned of unspecified action by the state. He mentioned Spro-cas and myself in this regard. A short while later, 40 security police raided Diakonia House, which housed, amongst other organizations, the Christian Institute, the SA Council of Churches and Ravan Press. The building was sealed off and every office was searched. In the case of Ravan, eight officers spent three hours perusing every document. They removed copies of *Black Review*, a dictionary and the Shell Company's *Guide to South Africa*.

In the face of both financial stringency and police harassment it seemed doubtful that Ravan would be able to continue for much longer. It was in this context that two developments occurred that were to shape the future of both Ravan and myself. In the first place, the University of the Witwatersrand offered me a temporary post in the Faculty of Education (my original training was as a teacher and I had taught at primary and secondary level in both Natal and England and had also lectured at the Natal Teachers' Training College). In the second place, the enigmatic Walter Felgate, who had secured the confidence of Beyers Naudé and was playing an important, if somewhat mysterious, role in the Christian Institute and related bodies, offered to inject working capital into Ravan and to relieve me of the administrative burden, thus freeing me to function as editor and publisher.

Both offers were gratefully accepted. I combined my university work with editing and publishing for Ravan, Felgate effectively became the business manager of the company, the staff increased and several new titles were produced. I decided to put political activism behind me and to concentrate on my new dual role. Felgate recruited Mike Kirkwood from the English Department of the University of Natal to join the editorial team. Thus, when the axe fell and I was banned in October 1977, together with all those individuals, organizations and newspapers that Minister Kruger had suspected of fomenting Black Consciousness, new people and a new structure were in place to carry Ravan forward. It was to be a very different Ravan, but that is a story that others must tell.

Glenn Moss

Ringing the changes –
*Twenty-five years of Ravan Press**

Indifference is the worst response any publisher can face. When the various constituencies – authors, readers, critics, booksellers, competitors – cease to care, then it's time to stop the presses.

Thankfully, in its first twenty-five years of existence, Ravan Press has provoked the fiercest of criticism, the strongest of loyalties, the greatest of conflicts. Its authors, directors and staff members have been banned, its books impounded, its offices fire-bombed. Education authorities, supported by fundamentalist religions, have withdrawn Ravan books from classrooms. It has published books which have broken new ground, challenged the old order, irritated new elites, won prestigious awards – and embarrassed supporters, trustees and staff alike!

For some, Ravan will always be associated with pathbreaking literature, poetry and drama – especially during the 1970s and first half of the 1980s. For others, Ravan is the pre-eminent publisher of both academic and popular history. Yet another group associates Ravan with contemporary social and political publishing to the left of South Africa's narrow political spectrum. But there are also those who, when they think of Ravan, identify biography and autobiography, or theology, or education, or children's literature, or literacy, or labour studies, or academic psychology, or gender studies.

I joined this controversial institution as "manager" (soon elevated to "managing director") in 1988. One of my first acts involved an unsuccessful attempt to purchase a desk (the size of the bank overdraft halted that initiative); soon after, I was forced to rid Ravan of the night services of a guard and large dog who jointly protected its offices from recurrent attempts to burn them down; not very much later, I recommended to senior Ravan trustees that closure was a more viable option than rescue, given the financial circumstances.

Flying back from London on old year's night, 1988, I penned my letter of resignation. Meetings with donors, authors and supporters on both sides of the Atlantic had convinced me that Ravan could not survive changes in the international and national climate; that its weaknesses as a publishing *company* were the direct results of its strengths as a socially-engaged and committed *publisher*; and that its internal systems in all the basics of publishing – warehousing, marketing, financial management, planning, sales representation – were so flawed as to defy restructuring.

Eight years later, when I finally left Ravan as managing director, this strange company which has a bird as a logo, but spells the name of that bird somewhat idiosyncratically, had proved me wrong, just as it had confounded so many others.

Ravan Press was incorporated as a publishing company on 29 November 1972. The name is made up of elements of its three founders: Peter *R*andall, Danie *v*an Zyl, and Beyers *N*audé. Elsewhere in this volume, Peter Randall has written on the early years of Ravan – from the time of its inception until his banning, and the banning of Beyers Naudé, in October 1977. The next period in Ravan's history is closely associated with Mike Kirkwood, and he should be the one to chart and analyse its course. But the editor of this volume could not make contact with him, and it falls to me to consider some of the exciting highs and frustrating lows which characterized the second major phase of Ravan's history.

Politically and socially, the five years following the founding of Ravan Press were marked by both the rise of Black Consciousness and the trade union movement. These were crucial moments in South Africa's history, signalling that the period of political and cultural quiescence which followed the intense oppression of the 1960s was ending.

These early years of Ravan's publishing laid the foundations for an expansion in the range of publishing undertaken, especially in the areas of fiction and poetry. Ravan was soon established as the main vehicle for an emerging group of creative writers – predominantly, but by no means exclusively black – whose works would otherwise not have seen publication.

The banning of Randall and Naudé in October 1977, together with other leading members of the Christian Institute, Black Consciousness groups and a range of organizations and media, brought this phase of Ravan's development to an end. But the seeds for future growth and new directions had been laid and, although the specifics of the publishing began changing, the basic continuity of social commitment in publishing endured.

The next decade of Ravan's life saw remarkable publishing creativity and energy, and disaster so great that it came close to destroying the publishing house. In the field of literature, both *Staffrider* magazine and the *Staffrider* series of books released the enormous well of angry yet creative energies bottled up in South Africa's townships. A new literary genre, often involving both a window on township life and experience and a powerful political protest against apartheid in all its manifestations, developed rapidly, with Ravan authors such as Njabulo Ndebele, Mtutuzeli Matshoba, Achmat Dangor, Wally Serote, Ellen Kuzwayo and Mafika Gwala leading from the front.

At the same time, Ravan was involved in publication of the works of a group of more-established authors which a combination of apartheid ideology and crass commercialism had kept away from many South African readers. As a result, the writings of Es'kia Mphahlele, Can Themba, Nat Nakasa, Casey Motsitsi, Nadine Gordimer, JM Coetzee and Christopher Hope, to mention but a few

15

of Ravan's distinguished authors, appeared under Ravan's imprint during this period.

But it was also a time of intense community, political, intellectual and working-class revival and, as in the past, Ravan's publishing both prefigured, and reflected this. The embryonic labour movement of the 1970s gave birth to a vibrant and dynamic trade unionism, which culminated in the formation of the Congress of South African Trade Unions in the mid-1980s. A host of community and local-level political struggles and organizations gave rise to the national launch of the United Democratic Front in August 1983. Ongoing township-based resistance to apartheid rule, especially in areas associated with rents and services, transport and education, and the forms of state control and repression aimed at countering this wave, left the foundations of society even more fragile than before. The tradition of politics broadly associated with the African National Congress and its historical allies – known as the "Congress" or "Charterist" tendency – began to dominate resistance and opposition politics.

This was the context in which Ravan published critical, reflective and radical studies of both contemporary South African society and its history. Popular and academic history; labour studies and books for workers; reinterpretive history of black politics, resistance and struggle; views and analysis of the Freedom Charter in South African history; a contemporary history of the trade union movement; new histories of the Xhosa, Zulu, Pedi, Tswana and Swazi peoples before white domination and colonization; Gandhi's place in South African politics; the Inkatha movement and KwaZulu politics; a radical critique of the Anglo-American empire; a subtle analysis and history of Afrikaner nationalism and its relationship to Afrikaner capitalism. Ravan was casting a probing light onto every aspect of social existence with the aim of interpreting, analysing, understanding and subjecting everything to a radical reassessment.

A second, slightly calmer area of publishing co-existed with the immediacy of social critique. Quality books for South Africa's children, free of the influences of racism, sexism and Euro-centrism gradually emerged as a larger area of Ravan's publishing programme

– although the publication of Marguerite Poland's classic, *The Mantis and the Moon*, in 1979, was an early signal of this direction. Literacy materials, and readings for the newly literate, skills for better language and writing for those learning English as a second language, and materials appropriate for supplementary use in school and non-formal education, slowly and quietly entered Ravan's list. Often unacknowledged and undervalued at the time – especially by library and educational authorities steeped in traditions of conservatism and blinkered by years of apartheid – many of these books have yet to take their rightful place in classrooms and on shelves.

Shares in Ravan were, in most cases, held effectively as a trusteeship. Individuals holding shares, in general, neither put capital into the publishing house, nor did they expect a financial return. During 1984, this position was formalised with the creation of the Ravan Trust, a body made up of noteworthy and credible figures from a range of areas who undertook both to guide Ravan's overall policy, and hold the majority of its shares as trustees.

Authors were strongly represented amongst the trustees: Achmat Dangor, Ahmed Essop, Nadine Gordimer, Chabani Manganyi, Njabulo Ndebele and Chris van Wyk. Ravan's theological origins were represented by Beyers Naudé and Desmond Tutu, while publishing for the academic community – an area in which Ravan was increasingly involved – was reflected in the appointment of historian Peter Delius and sociologist Eddie Webster as trustees. The key person in Ravan's foundation and first years of operation – Peter Randall, now unbanned – and his successor, Mike Kirkwood, made up the remaining trustees.

Kirkwood, who had succeeded Peter Randall as both publisher and managing director, presided over Ravan's expansion and new directions during the last part of the 1970s, and into the 1980s. Intensely creative, with a fine eye for potential in a manuscript, Kirkwood had built Ravan's list in an impressive manner. Working with a talented younger generation of editors who were often also authors — Ivan Vladislavić and Chris van Wyk come particularly to mind — remarkable books flowed from the press, firmly establishing Ravan at the cutting edge of critical, creative and socially committed publishing.

But the context in which Ravan operated was an exceptionally difficult one. The industry as a whole tended to be at best indifferent to the contribution being made — a contribution which demonstrated the narrowness, conservatism and lack of insight of most other publishers and many booksellers; at its worst, the book industry was hostile to Ravan and its initiatives. The state and its various organs were predictably antagonistic to Ravan, and this manifested itself in repetitive banning and confiscation of books, general harassment and intimidation, interference in the infrastructure necessary for normal business operations (telephones, postage, relations with printers), and physical attacks on Ravan premises and property.

In this regard, it is worth noting that the support Ravan did receive during this period — moral, financial and other — tended to come from publishers outside of South Africa, and progressive church-linked and development agencies which saw the value of Ravan's work. It is a blot on the history of South African publishing that so little support was forthcoming from within the industry itself.

In addition, Ravan's extremely limited financial resources meant that the hard skills necessary to run the business side of a publishing venture were difficult to acquire. Those who worked for Ravan - and they included some of the most talented editors and publishers South Africa has produced — often found themselves forced into roles not appropriate to their skills, interests and commitments.

Kirkwood had an immense literary and publishing talent. But he was increasingly forced into other roles: apart from functioning as publisher, editor and commissioning editor, he had to liaise with authors and other publishers, negotiate rights, raise funds, report to donors, motivate staff, set and enforce publishing standards, mediate in personnel conflicts, etc. In a classic small-organization conundrum, he was expected both to *manage* and *deliver* "products". This left increasingly less time for strategic and organizational planning.

Exhausted emotionally, intellectually and physically, Kirkwood resolved to restructure Ravan along supposedly "democratic" and "participatory" lines, dispensing with all hierarchy, and instituting a staff collective as Ravan's day-to-day governing body.

This was certainly in line with general egalitarian thinking in the broad movement opposed to apartheid, which Ravan identified with strongly. However, regardless of the validity of the ideas behind this experiment, it led to the progressive collapse of Ravan's internal structures, administration and staff morale. Conflicts surfaced, those professional and business elements necessary for the development of any publishing initiative, regardless of the content and ideological motivation, slipped into disarray, and Ravan slowly lost the pre-eminence and some of the respect which it had once enjoyed in its areas of publishing.

Disaffected authors began leaving Ravan, financial administration and control collapsed, and both financial and other disasters overtook the organization. Kirkwood left to start a new life in England, editors like Van Wyk and Vladislavić resigned from the staff (although they retained close links with Ravan as freelance editors or authors), and the pride of South African publishing stumbled closer and closer to collapse.

This was the context in which, after a brief and problematic interregnum involving a management consultant employed to run Ravan, the Ravan Trust resolved to constitute a more conventional hierarchy and invited me to join Ravan as its manager and publisher.

Ravan began the process of restructuring, reassessment and reconstitution at much the same time as the socio-political fabric of South Africa itself began to change dramatically.

The events symbolically associated with February 1990 radically altered the terrain within which progressive, indigenous anti-apartheid publishing took place. Almost overnight, some of the symbols, issues and modes of operation which had influenced nearly two decades of oppositional publishing seemed inappropriate. Some of the principles which had guided much of Ravan's publishing – especially in the fields of fiction and contemporary politics – faced the danger of becoming anachronistic in the new context.

Ultimately, Ravan's first two decades were dominated by an ethos of opposition – to apartheid, to intellectual intolerance, to gross exploitation of legally defenceless workers, to brutality by police and other repressive state forces, to corrupt and conceptually deforming educational structures, to the mediocrity and lack of vision which dominated so many of the major institutions which held power in society.

But the 1990s brought a whole range of new challenges, based fundamentally on critical engagement with, rather than simple opposition to, the mainstream of society. To some extent, this also involved consideration of publishing for reconstruction and transformation, rather than opposition.

Twenty-five years on, Ravan remains committed to publishing which is critical, socially relevant and of quality. But the 1990s have not been kind to publishing in general, or Ravan in particular.

Many of the factors with which Ravan has had to contend exist in the macro-environment, rather than within publishing itself. This has limited Ravan's options for development and expansion, although a number of important initiatives have been undertaken despite the narrow parameters imposed by external circumstances.

Sales of serious, critical books of quality to the public through retail outlets have declined for all publishers. The other two major markets for books in South Africa – educational and academic – have been fraught with difficulties associated with transition and restructuring.

But, in the early 1990s, Ravan felt upbeat about its future. From near-collapse, it had become a small but integrated publishing venture. Editing, typesetting and design, marketing, warehousing and distribution, invoicing, financial control and management were all undertaken in-house. While retaining a strong commitment to social publishing, Ravan had set up what appeared to be sound and efficient business principles. New staff had developed sound all-round publishing skills, and were increasingly becoming acknowledged and respected practitioners in their specific fields of expertise.

But purchasing – and perhaps even reading – of serious books of quality by the general public was declining considerably:
- hard economic times were limiting discretionary disposable income for most traditional book buyers;
- independent and specialist booksellers throughout the country began failing, with a number of traditional outlets for Ravan titles falling to closure or takeover by larger book chains;
- booksellers began stocking fewer and fewer backlist titles, and by the mid-1990s no single outlet stocked a reasonably representative sample of any publishers' titles.

Difficulties also emerged in the area of academic and tertiary publishing. Traditionally, Ravan had published a large number of social science and historical titles aimed specifically at university courses, institutions, libraries and lecturers. But a number of factors coalesced to limit this area:
- prescription of fewer and fewer texts for students, and their substitution with course readers;
- very low ceilings placed on multiple-copy orders for university library holdings;
- photocopying of books, or sections of books, both with and without permission, became endemic within universities, posing a serious threat to publishing in this area;
- lack of available funds for students to purchase books, whether these are prescribed or not.

Ravan attempted to respond to these difficulties creatively. It originated, in consultation with lecturers and departments, price-sensitive readers aimed at filling specific gaps in the teaching of courses. It offered texts at reduced prices directly to students, in co-operation with lecturers.

In collaboration with David Philip Publishers, Skotaville, the READ Trust and Learn and Teach Publications, Ravan was involved in an initiative to place copies of existing titles in a range of school and community libraries. Donors were sought to subsidize this scheme, while participating publishers offered very substantial discounts on titles selected for this scheme. READ assisted in assessment of titles, provided lists of appropriate library recipients for such books, and organized cataloguing, library processing, reinforcing and delivery of the books. The response from recipient libraries has been exceptionally positive.

But it became increasingly common cause, both in the publishing community in South Africa and elsewhere, that it was virtually impossible for indigenous, socially committed and engaged general publishing to create a viable base while operating on broadly commercial principles, and in a market economy.

For a period, Ravan believed that the most promising way of meeting these challenges lay in entry into the field of educational publishing. A few notable successes were achieved in the mid-1990s, when Ravan titles were prescribed for classroom use in large numbers. But the capital required to compete against existing educational publishers, which had built up enormous reserves through successful publishing for apartheid education, could not be accessed. By 1994, Ravan no longer believed that cross-subsidisation between educational and general publishing could be achieved.

Like many other indigenous publishers of quality, Ravan increasingly faced competition from hugely resourced multinational publishers; from book imports; and from the efforts of those local publishers who had built their operations on privileged access to the discredited departments and systems of education.

The last few years I spent in Ravan were witness to some remarkable moments. Ravan authors had, over the years, received more awards for their books than any other South African publisher. Continuing this tradition into the first half of the 1990s, Ravan authors featured prominently in the CNA Literary Awards, the *Sunday Times* Alan Paton Prize and the Noma Award for Publishing in Africa.

Working closely in an increasingly warm relationship with David Philip Publishers, Ravan was prominent in the formation and consolidation of the Independent Publishers' Association of South Africa (IPASA), the African Publishers' Network (APNET), and the unified Publishers' Association of South Africa (PASA).

Book launches involving Nelson Mandela as guest of honour were remarkable events: one culminated in a massive celebration in the precinct of the Market Theatre's Newtown complex, with thousands dancing to the music of the African Jazz Pioneers. Another, more dignified occasion (Mandela was now state president) launched the unfinished autobiography of Joe Slovo before an impressive array of South Africans who had committed their lives to opposing apartheid.

For me, personally, two visits to the Frankfurt Book Fair as a guest of the German government – once representing Ravan, once South African publishing more broadly – were particularly fascinating. It was here that I discovered the international dimension to publishing, and learned that difficulties which seemed unique were, in truth, part of a global process.

By 1994, the Ravan Trust had agreed to sell a majority of its shares to a commercial partner. This followed recommendations from Ravan's senior staff, including me. Donor funding for publishing was drying up; markets were shrinking; South African publishing was in transition.

Each major phase of Ravan's history had been presided over by a different figure. Peter Randall in the early and mid-1970s; Mike Kirkwood in the late 1970s to late 1980s; and I had the privilege of restructuring and leading Ravan in some of South Africa's most turbulent but exciting times, when the socio-political ideals which Ravan had always stood for began to reach fulfilment in the broader society.

Ravan had always been sensitive to nuances and developments in society. Transformation was in the air and, for Ravan, it was again time for change!

*Many have contributed much to Ravan Press – authors, donors, trustees and others. But a special tribute is due to those who staffed the publishing house over the years, usually for very little material reward. In particular, this article is in tribute to those who I worked with most closely during my period as managing director: Monica Seeber, who was a skilled and highly competent deputy; Ingrid Obery, who ran Ravan's production; and Ipuseng Kotsokoane, in charge of sales and marketing.

Albert Grundlingh
Publishing the Past: Ravan Press and Historical Writing

In November 1996 when it was assumed (wrongly) that Ravan Press was about to be closed down, Tony Morphet, formerly from the University of Natal and currently from the University of Cape Town, suggested that it might be a worthwhile idea "to let some really good historian into the archives to tell the full life and times of the bird and the book. It might just be the best book of the lot".[1] That project awaits another historian and another time. Apart from my shortcomings as an historian, I cannot claim an intimate acquaintance with the internal history of Ravan or the inner circle of people who sustained its extraordinary publishing drive. Having studied at predominantly Afrikaans institutions during the apartheid years, one's academic socialization and career trajectory followed a different path from those who graduated from English-speaking South African universities or British and American universities, and who formed the core group of academics associated with Ravan. Although some of my work has been published by Ravan, I do find myself more in the position of an outsider looking in than the other way round. Such a perspective has its advantages and disadvantages; others, I am sure, would have written a different appreciation of Ravan's contribution to South African historical writing. All this brief exposition can do, is to provide a preliminary outline of the topic, interspersed with some personal impressions of Ravan during the "struggle years".

Little research has been done in South Africa on the cultural brokering role of publishing houses in the dissemination of historical and political ideologies. In the Canadian context though, it has been noted that "printed publications – nearly always express the conscious part of culture, willed, proscribed and distilled by elite groups for the mass market. Publishing is a vehicle for ideology, for symbol-building ..."[2] Much the same principle can be seen to apply in South Africa; before the advent of electronic media in South Africa, publishers occupied a pre-eminent position either as ideological facilitators or as gatekeepers. The cultural and political rise of Afrikaner nationalism from the 1940s to the 1960s owes much to a publishing house like Nasionale Pers. In many of its historical publications, history was presented in such a way that it formed one of the cornerstones of the nationalist project. A strong Afrikanercentric vision of the past was propagated in different formats: brochures, pamphlets, popular history books, academic works, documentary publications, historical novels, dramas and pictorial presentations. As CFJ Muller, the historian of Nasionale Pers, concludes, the publishing house "made sure that the history of the Afrikaner, by the Afrikaner, for the Afrikaner and in Afrikaans, saw the light of day, at times under difficult conditions, and gained greater recognition".[3] The Afrikaner version of the past, however flawed, certainly succeeded in making its mark, and till well into the 1980s it was the main historical tradition that fed into school history textbooks and that the great majority of literate South Africans were exposed to in print.[4]

Censorship on the one hand and political apathy on the other, saw to it that on the whole the mainstream English language publishing houses failed to oppose vigorously the way in which Afrikaners had appropriated the past to shore up narrow nationalistic ideals and buttress apartheid. Admittedly, from time to time publishers like Oxford University Press produced books which could be construed as opposing the prevailing orthodoxy, but the publishing house was also rather timid. After taking legal advice it self-censured a chapter by Leo Kuper on African nationalism in South Africa between 1910 and 1964 in the South African edition of the *Oxford History of South Africa*, (1971) edited by Monica Wilson and Leonard Thompson. Blank pages in these volumes where the chapter on African politics was supposed to be, sought to make a symbolic political point; from the perspectives of the 1990s these pages probably tell us more about the publisher than the apartheid government. Such was the state of play in the early 1970s when Ravan was born and about to spread its wings. Apart from David Philip in Cape Town which started up at more or less the same time, there was not one publishing house in the country dedicated to publishing alternative texts, critical of the *status quo*, on an on-going basis.

No intellectual project proceeds in a vacuum and Ravan, destined to become an important contributor in the cultural and political marketplace, was very much a product of its time. In wider South African society in the 1970s the apparent quiescence of the black population during the previous decade of high apartheid, was to give way to increasing labour and political unrest. The 1973 strikes of black workers in Durban in particular, set the scene for gradual changes on the labour front. Of significance was also an unusually close interaction between certain academics and the labour movement which helped to emphasize a modified set of categories through which the prevailing South African reality could be refracted. Instead of concentrating on the salience of racial attitudes, neo-Marxian structural analysis of South Africa began to emerge which stressed the role of economic forces and labour in social relations. Particularly influential in this respect was Rick Turner of the University of Natal who confronted the English-speaking "hippie" and surfing student generation in Durban with uncomfortable notions that apartheid was more than just an Afrikaner invention and that the role of English-speaking capitalists should not be left out of the equation. Turner's book, *The eye of the needle: towards participatory democracy in South Africa* (1972) was one of the first pioneering texts of a new generation of scholars to be published under the Ravan imprint. Dissident ideas which could be construed as communist, combined with a measure of political activism were dangerous; fatefully so as Turner was assassinated by agents of the state in 1978.

In the same cohort as Turner was an English lecturer at the

University of Natal, Mike Kirkwood, who edited what has been described as a "quirky little literary mag", called *Bolt*[5]. Kirkwood was to join Ravan in 1977 and it had been claimed that some of the ideas that he brought to Ravan has first been seeded in *Bolt*. One of them was that the "Marxist historians not only had great things to say about the country, but that they also made better reading than most novels".[6] Kirkwood was also concerned about the distortions and gaps in South African historical writing and the perceived pusillanimity of Oxford University Press to excise the chapter on black politics in the South African edition of their product.[7]

The ensuing years saw a great number of history titles appearing. At least 30 per cent of all Ravan's publications were on history or history-related topics and many of them appeared under the sub-title, "New History of Southern African Series".[8] It would be tedious to list all the titles, but any overview will be incomplete without at least mentioning some of the historians who have been associated with Ravan over the past 25 years: Jeff Guy with his work on the destruction of the Zulu kingdom, Jeff Peires on Xhosa history, Peter Delius on the Pedi polity, Phil Bonner on the evolution and dissolution of the 19th century Swazi state, Colin Bundy and William Beinart on popular movements in the Eastern Cape between 1890 and 1930, Eddie Webster on trade unionism, Tom Lodge on 20th century black politics, Tim Keegan on rural change on the Highveld, Helen Bradford on the dynamics and social character of the Industrial and Commercial Workers' Union of the 1920s, Dan O'Meara on the class dimensions of Afrikaner politics, and Belinda Bozzoli on the lives of women in a rural settlement in the former homeland of Bophuthatswana. Ravan also had in its stable the foremost South African social historian and master stylist, Charles van Onselen, who wrote on the underclasses of the Witwatersrand after the discovery of gold in 1886.

Ravan titles covered different dimensions of history, but it is probably fair to say that the social history genre with its emphasis on the impact of socio-economic forces on the lives of ordinary people tend to dominate. Social historians focused on groupings on the periphery of society which had not been deemed worthy of investigation by an earlier and more conventional historiography. While the latter concentrated on developments in white politics, policy matters and the "big (white) men" of the South African past, social historians brought onto the historical stage hitherto forgotten actors: criminal gangs, migrants, township dwellers, domestic workers, cab drivers, prostitutes, "poor whites" and a host of other marginalized groups and little known social movements.

The clearing house for much social history was the History Workshop at the University of the Witwatersrand which, from 1978 to 1994, held regular tri-ennial conferences. A particularly close relationship developed between Ravan and the Workshop, and Ravan regularly published edited volumes of essays drawn from the History Workshop conferences. The first edition appeared in 1979 under the title *Labour, township and protest: Studies in the social history of the Witwatersrand.* One of the features of this series was the thought-provoking editorial introductions often written by Belinda Bozzoli; apart from perceptive comments on the essays in the volumes, she also provided meta-perspectives on the theory and nature of historical discourse at the time.

Besides its academic publishing, Ravan, in conjunction with the History Workshop, sought to popularise new historical interpretations. Collecting and distilling insights from academic books into a more user-friendly format had its own set of demands. Luli Callinicos who was entrusted with the task explained that "the writers of popular history have to be particularly scrupulous in researching sources and analysing them – partly because the populariser has a responsibility to pursue careful and thoughtful scholarship on behalf of readers who might not have the resources to follow up the research, but also because, like academic radical scholarship, their work is apt to be subjected to sharp attacks by hostile critics (always very useful for concentrating the mind!)".[9] Callinicos certainly took these requirements to heart and produced popular histories that were models of conceptual clarity and accessibility. One of them, *Working Life*, (1986) was awarded with the Noma prize for publications from Africa.

Other popular histories also appeared: Paul la Hausse on the politics of liquor in South Africa and Robert Edgar on the Israelites, the millenarian sect at Bulhoek near Queenstown which suffered heavily as numbers of them were mowed down by the police in 1921. Dealing with a dramatic event such as Bulhoek, Edgar was careful not to romanticize the tragic event, but sought to contextualize and humanize the movement. Among the current descendants of the Israelites the booklet has been well received and has added substance to historical memory.[10]

Ravan's prodigious output of historical works was made possible, in large part, by generous foreign funding. An analysis of the ramifications of donor funding on cultural production still needs to be done by an enterprising scholar, taking due account not only of the economic base but also human agency. What struck me during my, admittedly brief encounters with Ravan staffers during the 1980s, was the commitment to alternative publishing. Perhaps deliberately in keeping with a socialist image, Ravan offices were situated in a rather run-down 1930s style house with an overgrown garden in O'Reilly Street, Berea. Mike Kirkwood, a tall and big-boned man, eschewed the traditional suit-and-tie attire of the business world, and casually dressed with a red bandana draped around the neck he looked the part of a socialist publisher. I found him an open and supportive person, and at the time this was well appreciated as my manuscript on South African black people and the First World War had a rather twisted and trying pre-history before it found its way to Ravan. Besides Kirkwood, there was Ivan Vladislavić, a noted novelist, who stands out in my memory as an excellent editor. As an outsider one gained the impression that the operation was being run without a visible formal hierarchical order; no sumptuous offices for directors and often decisions were taken while sitting on a wooden bench in the backyard. Furthermore, there was the realization on my part that anti-apartheid publishing during the successive states of emergencies in the 1980s ran real risks as part of the Ravan offices were firebombed. This necessitated that some staff members had to move into nearby flats with heavy security gates. Perhaps my overriding impression of Ravan during these years was that there was a common sense of camaraderie in the face of outside threats. It was only later that I learnt that like in most other organisations, there was also considerable tension underneath the surface.

What was the impact of Ravan's historical publications? It is always difficult to quantify the influence of ideas and books; the question goes beyond the number of copies sold. The best one can do is to convey certain impressionistic evidence. It would not be too much to claim that Ravan authors and to a certain extent also those associated with David Philip, had significantly altered the general landscape of academic South African historiography and the contents of what was being taught in the lecture halls. Few arts students graduated from traditional English-speaking campuses without having perused at least one Ravan publication. Moreover, at conferences and other academic meetings, ideas emanating from Ravan books were often in circulation. Phil Bonner of the University of the Witwatersrand and closely associated with both the History Workshop and Ravan, certainly had sufficient reason to state recently that the academic publications from this quarter had "a major impact on the writing of the South African history and on South African students".[11] While Ravan authors undoubtedly led the general academic field in the 1980s, historians on Afrikaans-speaking campuses and history lecturers at black homeland universities, with a few notable exceptions, were, mainly for political reasons, resistant to the changes which engulfed their discipline.[12]

Outside of academe, certain Ravan publications were deemed to have an influence on black political consciousness. Whether this was indeed the case though, is problematical. In 1976 during a trial of Black Consciousness leaders the state claimed that the concepts in Rick Turner's work of 1972 had influenced the accused.[13] This probably had as much, if not more, to do with state paranoia and a belief that black people were incapable of formulating their own opposition to apartheid, than it had to do with the academic contents of Turner's book. Turner's exposition cannot easily be construed as a blueprint for the Black Consciousness philosophy as he incorporated considerably more than race in the analysis of the apartheid system.

Ravan publications did much to rephrase the debate about the South African past and to bring into focus earlier struggles against oppression. Some of this fed into the Anti-Apartheid Movement's campaign abroad where "cutting-edge radical historiography was used to highlight and explain facets of apartheid".[14] It does not, however, appear that Ravan history books were widely used by the African National Congress in exile. At the Solomon Mahlangu Freedom College in Tanzania where John Pampallis taught history, he had to rely on outdated texts and in desperation he decided upon compiling his own book. Conditions in exile complicated the acquisition of new literature and it was only while doing research in England in the latter part of the 1980s that he readily came into contact with Ravan publications. In preparing and revising his manuscript for publication under the Maskew Miller/Longman imprint in 1991, he was, interestingly enough, assisted by Mike Kirkwood who by then had left Ravan and emigrated to England.[15]

We have already noted how Edgar's booklet on the Israelites seems to have found a wider audience. Ravan history texts also made their mark in the public domain in rather unexpected ways. Luli Callinicos has recounted how Phil Bonner's academic analysis of 19th century Swaziland caught the attention of a man delivering goods at Ravan's offices. He bought the book and returned several times to discuss its contents. With little formal schooling he slowly went through the book and underlined references to his clan, and in the process discovered some long lost clan members.[16]

Overall, Ravan history texts seem to have had an uneven impact. Its influence on academic life was, and is, indisputable and its more popular history books received well deserved recognition, but as a publishing house Ravan never became a major player in the mass market. Neither did it shift a gear up (or down) in an attempt to move into the production of school history textbooks. There were, of course, problems in this regard like strict government controls over syllabuses and vested interests of other publishing houses in the school market. It is somewhat ironic though, that now that the country is in a process of democratization, a new state which was able to draw considerable strengths from the past in its fight against apartheid, has decided that history is no longer that important and in the new Curriculum 2005 it has been scaled down quite significantly as a school subject. This means that many of the ideas that have been seeded by Ravan history texts, will not come to full bloom in the classrooms of the new South Africa.

Apart from other considerations, one also suspects that the historical ideology which Ravan had propagated – and most of the Ravan authors will readily admit that it was and is an ideology – will not easily meet current ideological requirements comprising, amongst a host of elements, a fluid amalgam of big business and black nationalism. Although Ravan authors did much to uncover African history, theirs was an approach informed by critical class analysis and a healthy suspicion of all nationalist movements, white or black. As such, its basic point of departure is potentially as damaging to the new elite as it was to the old. Also in the academic market place Ravan's shares are no longer what they used to be as postmodernist notions of history on the one hand, and self-consciously and at times shrill Africanist interpretations of the past on the other, are tentatively probing the continuing validity of the social history paradigm.[17]

During the 1970s and 1980s, Ravan authors contributed to a considerable expansion in the scope of historical enquiry and the nature of our understanding the past. But for various reasons, many of them beyond the control of the publishing house, Ravan left no natural progeny. Despite a complex set of explanations which can be advanced to explain this state of affairs, it has to be recognized that structurally historical writing during the apartheid years took place in a kind of a vacuum and that some of the potential contributors to the debate were absent. In this respect it has been remarked recently that "black consciousness intellectuals made no systematic effort to rewrite history or demolish the canons of colonial historiography, although they made occasional references to the need to do so. The need to change the future proved too compelling, and the task of changing the past was left to radical white academics."[18] Now the situation has changed. With a new political dispensation in place and formal anti-apartheid struggles officially part of history, a younger generation of black scholars is in the process of slowly starting to fill academic posts, and they will, in many cases, be the recipients of the received wisdom of Ravan publications. It is a scholarship that they, coming from a different background than many of the predominantly white Ravan historians, will have to engage with academically, and either reject (full or partially) or accept (fully or partially) and perhaps build upon or refine. The outcome of this process will, in part at least, depend on the wider academic and cultural environment of critical interchange of ideas in the South Africa of today and tomorrow. And this in turn, will to some extent have a bearing on the future direction of Ravan.

1. *Weekly Mail & Guardian*, 1 November to 7 November 1996, 'Ravan: child of a special time.'
2. LM Cole, *Archival gold* (Vancouver, 1989) p. viii.
3. CFJ Muller, *Sonop in die suide: gehoorte en groei van die Nasionale Pers, 1915 – 1948* (Cape Town, 1990) p. 557
4. WM Friend, 'Past Imperfect', *Southern African Review of Books*, December/January 1989.
5. *Weekly Mail & Guardian*, 1 November to 7 November 1996, 'Ravan: child of a special time.'
6. *Weekly Mail & Guardian*, 1 November to 7 November 1996, 'Ravan: child of a special time.'
7. *Bolt*, 5, 1971, p. 1.
8. Ravan Catalogue, 1996.
9. L Callinicos, 'The peoples' past: Towards transforming the present', *Critical Arts*, 4, 2, 1986, p. 2.
10. R Edgar, 'Writing because they chose the plan of God', *Perspectives in Education*, 12, 1990, pp. 121–124; Interview with Robert Edgar, 5 August 1997.
11. P Bonner, 'New Nation, New History: The History Workshop in South Africa, 1977–1994', *The Journal of American History*, December 1994, p. 979. See also B Bozzoli and P Delius, 'Radical history and South African society', *Radical History Review*, 46/7, 1990, pp. 20–23.
12. Compare A Grundlingh, 'Sosiale geskiedenis en die dilemma in Afrikanergeskiedskrywing', *South African Historical Journal*, 19, 1987, pp. 31–49.
13. R Turner, *The eye of the needle: towards participatory democracy in South Africa*. (Johannesburg, 1980 reprint with an introduction by Tony Morphet), p. vii–viii.
14. H South Africa Net, 17 January 1997, Communication from Peter Limb.
15. J Pampallis, *Foundations of the New South Africa* (Cape Town, 1991), Acknowledgements and Foreword; Interview with John Pampallis, 5 July 1995.
16. L Callinicos, 'The peoples' past: Towards transforming the present', *Critical Arts*, 4, 2, 1986, p. 38 n 16.

17. This is discussed in greater detail in A Grundlingh, 'Transcending Transitions? The social history tradition of historical writing in South Africa in the 1990's', Inaugural lecture, University of South Africa, 1997.
18. TG Karis and GM Gerhart (Eds.) *From protest to challenge: a documentary history of African politics in South Africa, 1882–1990*, vol 5, *Nadir and resistance, 1964–1979*. (Pretoria, 1997), p. 108.

PART 2
New Writing

J M Coetzee
Boyhood

There is a telephone call from Cape Town. Aunt Annie has had a fall on the steps of her flat in Rosebank. She had been taken to hospital with a broken hip; someone must come and make arrangements for her.

It is July, mid-winter. Over the whole of the Western Cape there is a blanket of cold and rain. They catch the morning train to Cape Town, he and his mother and his brother, then a bus up Kloof Street to the Volkshospitaal. Aunt Annie, tiny as a baby in her flowered nightdress, is in the female ward. The ward is full: old women with cross, pinched faces shuffling about in their dressing-gowns, hissing to themselves; fat, blowsy women with vacant faces sitting on the edges of their beds, their breasts carelessly spilling out. A loudspeaker in the corner plays Springbok Radio. Three o'clock, the afternoon request programme: "When Irish Eyes are Smiling", Nelson Riddle and his orchestra.

Aunt Annie takes his mother's arm in a wizened grip. 'I want to leave this place, Vera,' she says in a hoarse whisper. 'It is not the place for me.'

His mother pats her hand, tries to soothe her. On the bedside table, a glass of water for her teeth and a Bible.

The ward sister tells them that the broken hip has been set. Aunt Annie will have to spend another month in bed while the bone knits. 'She's not young any more, it takes time.' After that she will have to use a crutch.

As an afterthought the sister adds that when Aunt Annie was

brought in her toenails were as long and black as birdclaws.

His brother, bored, has begun to whine. He complains he is thirsty. His mother stops a nurse and persuades her to fetch a glass of water. Embarrassed, he looks away.

They are sent down the corridor to the social worker's office. 'Are you the relatives?' says the social worker. 'Can you offer her a home?'

His mother's lips tighten. She shakes her head.

'Why can't she go back to her flat?' he says to his mother afterwards.

'She can't climb the stairs. She can't get to the shops.'

'I don't want her to live with us.'

'She is not coming to live with us.'

The visiting-hour is over, it is time to say goodbye. Tears well up in Aunt Annie's eyes. She clutches his mother's arm so tightly that her fingers have to be prised loose.

'Ek wil huistoe gaan, Vera,' she whispers.

'Just a few days more, Aunt Annie, till you can walk again,' says his mother in her most soothing voice.

He has never seen this side of her before: this treacherousness.

Then it is his turn. Aunt Annie reaches out a hand. Aunt Annie is both his great-aunt and his godmother. In the album there is a photograph of her with a baby in her arms said to be him. She is wearing a black dress down to her ankles and an old-fashioned black hat; there is a church in the background. Because she is his godmother she believes she has a special relationship with him. She does not seem to pick up the disgust he feels for her, wrinkled and ugly in her hospital bed, the disgust he feels for this whole ward full of ugly women. He tries to keep his disgust from showing; his heart burns with shame. He endures the hand on his arm, but he wants to be gone, to be out of this place and never to come back.

'You are so clever,' says Aunt Annie in the low, hoarse voice she has had ever since he can remember. 'You are a big man, your mother depends on you. You must love her and be a support for her and for your little brother too.'

A support for his mother? What nonsense. His mother is like a rock, like a stone column. It is not he who must be a support for her, it is she who must be a support for him! Why is Aunt Annie saying these things anyhow? She is pretending she is going to die when all she has is a broken hip.

He nods, tries to look serious and attentive and obedient while secretly he is only waiting for her to let go of him. She smiles the meaningful smile that is meant to be a sign of the special bond between her and Vera's firstborn, a bond he does not feel at all, does not acknowledge. Her eyes are flat, pale blue, washed out. She is eighty years old and nearly blind. Even with glasses she cannot read the Bible properly, only hold it on her lap and murmur the words to herself.

She relaxes her grip; he mumbles something and retreats.

His brother's turn. His brother submits to being kissed.

'Goodbye, dear Vera,' croaks Aunt Annie. 'Mag die Here jou seën, jou en die kinders.'

It is five o'clock and beginning to get dark. In the unfamiliar bustle of the city rush-hour they catch a train to Rosebank. They are going to spend the night in Aunt Annie's flat: the prospect fills him with gloom.

Aunt Annie has no fridge. Her larder contains nothing but a few withered apples, a mouldy half-loaf of bread, a jar of fishpaste that his mother does not trust. She sends him out to the Indian shop; they have bread and jam and tea for supper.

The toilet bowl is brown with dirt. His stomach turns when he thinks of the old woman with the long black toenails squatting over it. He does not want to use it.

'Why have we got to stay here?' he asks. 'Why have we got to stay here?' echoes his brother. 'Because,' says his mother grimly.

Aunt Annie uses forty-watt bulbs to save electricity. In the dim yellow light of the bedroom his mother begins to pack Aunt Annie's clothes into cardboard boxes. He has never been into Aunt Annie's bedroom before. There are pictures on the wall, framed photographs of men and women with stiff, forbidding looks: Brechers, Du Biels, his ancestors.

'Why can't she go and live with Uncle Albert?'

'Because Kitty can't look after two sick old people.'

'I don't want her to live with us.'

'She is not going to live with us.'

'Then where is she going to live?'

'We will find a home for her.'

'What do you mean, a home?'

'A home, a home, a home for old people.'

The only room in Aunt Annie's flat that he likes is the storeroom. The storeroom is piled to the ceiling with old newspapers and carton boxes. There are shelves full of books, all the same: a squat book in a red binding, printed on the thick, coarse paper used for Afrikaans books that looks like blotting-paper with flecks of chaff and fly-dirt trapped in it. The title on the spine is *Ewige Genesing*; on the front cover is the full title, *Deur 'n Gevaarlike Krankheid tot Ewige Genesing*, Through a Dangerous Malady to Eternal Healing. The book was written by his great-grandfather, Aunt Annie's father; to it – he has heard the story many times – she has devoted most of her life, first translating the manuscript from German into Afrikaans, then spending her savings to pay a printer in Stellenbosch to print hundreds of copies, and a binder to bind some of them, then touring the bookshops of Cape Town. When the bookshops could not be persuaded to sell the book, she trudged from door to door herself. The leftovers are on the shelves here in the storeroom; the boxes contain folded, unbound printed pages.

He has tried to read *Ewige Genesing*, but it is too boring. No sooner has Balthazar du Biel got under way with the story of his boyhood in Germany than he interrupts it with long reports of lights in the sky and voices speaking to him out of the heavens. The whole of the book seems to be like that: short bits about himself followed by long recountings of what the voices told him. He and his father have longstanding jokes about Aunt Annie and her father Balthazar du Biel. They intone the title of his book in the sententious, sing-song manner of a predikant, drawing out the vowels: 'Deur 'n gevaaaarlike krannnnnkheid tot eeeewige geneeeeesing.'

'Was Aunt Annie's father mad?' he asks his mother.

'Yes, I suppose he was mad.'

'Then why did she spend all her money printing his book?'

'She was surely afraid of him. He was a terrible old German, terribly cruel and autocratic. All his children were afraid of him.'

'But wasn't he already dead?'

'Yes, he was dead, but she surely had a sense of duty toward him.'

She does not want to criticize Aunt Annie and her sense of duty toward the mad old man.

The best thing in the storeroom is the book press. It is made of iron as heavy and solid as the wheel of a locomotive. He persuades his brother to lay his arms in the bed of the press; then he turns the great screw until his arms are pinned and he cannot escape. After which they change places and his brother does the same to him.

One or two more turns, he thinks, and the bones will be crushed. What is it that makes them forbear, both of them?

'At least you can be proud to have someone in your family who did something with his life, who left something behind him,' says his mother.

'You said he was a horrible old man. You said he was cruel.'

'Yes, but he did something with his life.'

In the photograph in Aunt Annie's bedroom Balthazar du Biel has grim, staring eyes and a tight, harsh mouth. Beside him his wife looks tired and cross. Balthazar du Biel met her, the daughter of another missionary, when he came to South Africa to convert the heathen. Later, when he travelled to America to preach the gospel, he took her and their three children along. On a paddlesteamer on the Mississippi someone gave his daughter Annie an apple, which she brought to show him. He gave her a thrashing for having spoken to a stranger. These are the few facts he knows about Balthazar, plus what is contained in the clumsy red book of which there are many more copies in the world than the world wants.

Balthazar's three children are Annie, Louisa — his mother's mother — and Albert, who figures in the photographs in Aunt Annie's bedroom as a frightened-looking boy in a sailor suit. Now Albert is Uncle Albert, a bent old man with pulpy white flesh like a mushroom who trembles all the time and has to be supported as he walks. Uncle Albert has never earned a proper salary in his life. He has spent his days writing books and stories; his wife has been the one to go out and work.

He asks his mother about Uncle Albert's books. She read one long ago, she says, but cannot remember it. 'They are very old-fashioned. People don't read books like that any more.'

He finds two books by Uncle Albert in the storeroom, printed on the same thick paper as *Ewige Genesing* but bound in brown covers, the same brown as benches on railway stations. One is called *Kain*, the other *Die Sondes van die Vaders*, The Sins of the Fathers. 'Can I take them?' he asks his mother. 'I'm sure you can,' she says. 'No one is going to miss them.'

He tries to read *Die Sondes van die Vaders*, but does not get beyond page ten, it is too boring.

'You must love your mother and be a support for her.' He broods on Aunt Annie's instructions. Love: a word he mouths with distaste. He sees no sense in love. When men and women kiss in films, and violins play low and lush in the background, he squirms in his seat. He vows he will never be like that: soft, soppy.

Chris van Wyk
Four Poems

Granny

When I remember granny's house I remember paradise
where the almighty was always broke
but kept puffing up the deflated clouds
and mending the flagging harpstrings in the corner
of her room where the sun poured through the curtains
like the warm weak black tea that she liked to sip
while she listened to our disputes, kissed our bloody knees,
felt our foreheads for fevers that sometimes
crept into our games and knocked us out for days.

In the mornings – holidaying at my granny's –
all my cousins and I rose as one almost – from beds and
makeshift beds among the shoes and mice and drifted to the
warm kitchen where twenty cups stood like a fleet
of old cracked steamboats waiting for us to dip
our buttered bread into the sweet black brew.

And my cousins knew all the film stars, all the pop songs,
and some verses from the Bible that we learned
from the Salvation Army with their funny hats and
twangy voices and skins so white and frail that I did believe
if we were all fitted with our wings one day their shoulders
would never take the strain. They met us every Sunday under

a tree in Hamilton Street where they dispensed
with endless tracts of verse.

And often all of these, the verses and the
film stars and the pop songs came together
in one huge Mardi Gras that brought every braided girl
and snot-nosed boy from Fuel Road
to Riversdale into my very own granny's yard
so that my heart swelled and swelled to accommodate
all the love and merriment.

And once upon a holiday
I came for my umpteenth – but almost last time – to Granny's
and there was my cousin Richard with a new gun
and, without blinking, Granny, the fastest gun alive
snapped the symmetric plastic pistol in two; one for me
and one for Rich who didn't mind one bit.
Then we tamed the pillows into horses and shot each other
down until we both died laughing.

And once Granny – the fastest draw alive – took
guess who, because of all the cousins he was the
only one who loved to read,
to town to draw her pension.
And afterwards, at the second-hand bookshop,
two books that Granny helped me choose
by flipping through random pages
although much later I learned that the black words
on the white sheets that swept me across the seas
to adventures in faraway lands were to Granny
like coal strewn across a field of snow.

And now Granny's hair is turning silver
as the stars drop their tears on her head
begging her to come and live among them

in their own version of Paradise.
Granny has been resisting for so long now
but soon I know she'll give in as she always has
to all of us whose empty cups
she filled with dreams and golden tea.

My Mother's Laughter

When I think of my mother's laughter
and how it rang through my childhood
I search for a way to bring it to you
and the nearest analogy
of those sounds that slaughtered the sadness
is this:

When I loosened the string
that choked
my bag of marbles
and threw them onto the earth
they captured the sun in their prisms
even as they ran free
and transformed
their little windows of light
into coins that I squandered on joy
with all my friends

On Sundays my mother's laughter
swept the sombre crosses off
the shoulders of the churchgoers
flung us into the streets
with our white shirts
pockmarked with the talismans
of tomato sauce
and the brooches of beetroot

My mother's sheer laughter
filled the afternoon cheering
football fields
flew through the nets
of the goalposts
and the bags of the whistling
orange vendors

Throughout her life
my mother laughed
as she still does today
and even though there
was much to cry about
as there is even now
so seldom does she weep
that I am forced to put her tears
in parentheses

My mother's laughter grows
out of our house
and people come
to taste it
Citrus mirth
Deciduous pleasure
Evergreen

My mother's laughter runs in the family.

I Have my Father's Voice

When I walk into a room
where my father has just been
I fill the same spaces he did
from the elbows on the table
to the head thrown back
and when we laugh we aim the guffaw
at the same space in the air.
Before anybody has told me this I know
because I see myself through
my father's eyes.

When I was a pigeon-toed boy
my father used his voice
to send me to bed
to run and buy the newspaper
to scribble my way through matric.

He also used his voice for harsher things:
to bluster when we made a noise
when the kitchen wasn't cleaned after supper
when I was out too late.

Late for work, on many mornings,
one sock in hand, its twin
an angry glint in his eye he flings
dirty clothes out of the washing box:
vests, jeans, pants and shirts shouting
anagrams of fee fo fi fum until he is up
to his knees in a stinking heap of laundry.

I have my father's voice too
and his fuming temper
and I shout as he does.

But I spew the words out
in pairs of alliteration
and an air of assonance.

Everything a poet needs
my father has bequeathed me
except the words.

Aunty

Being some seventeen years
younger than my mother
Aunty was my childhood friend
running around among the boxcarts
that evolved out of broken prams
and clapping hands at
the birthdays
that snuffed out a
year of poverty
and lit a candle to another.

Somehow the years
solidified into decades,
calcified as I learnt
to fling words at them
to turn them into
what I wanted them to be
or not to be
with my romantic
little cuticles
and my fat fingers of fiction.

But the other day,
winter settling comfortably
into its cold threadbare evenings
I visited Aunty.
She was thin.
There were children everywhere,
bursting from her womb
and filling her tiny rooms
in their far-flung diaspora.

Aunty's life has been
a half circle of childhood

and a hemisphere of adulthood:
two identical halves,
of one perfect circle
that bubbles like
the solitary pot of pap
on her stove.

Mary Benson
Athol Fugard and the New South Africa

The text of Athol's first play to be written in the New South Africa began with the stage direction: "A small travelling amusement park encamped on the outskirts of a Karoo town." During my visit to Port Elizabeth in 1965 he had driven me to Korsten where once Morrie and Zach had lived and there, in the dusty squalor, was a garishly lit funfair PLAYLAND. When Lisa was a child, he said, he'd taken her to ride on its merry-go-round and swings and once he had noticed the black attendant of the "happiness machine" muttering to himself with a strange intensity, and he'd wondered whether the man might, in a fit of fury, speed up the machine. I came away with an image of the man, crazily laughing as he watched whites trapped in their seats and spinning faster and faster, beyond all control. Eagerly I awaited the play Athol would write with this character a metaphor for black rage.

Now *Playland* had been written and South African critics thought it "a masterpiece", "unforgettable vintage Fugard", "a play of effortless simplicity and vast thematic richness". When Athol brought his production to London in February 1993 that man was incarnated in Martinus who, however, far from being out of control, was a dignified, religious night-watchman at the funfair.

For Athol the catalyst in writing the play had been a photograph of white South African soldiers in Namibia dropping the corpses of black men from a truck into a crude hole. He'd imagined a black woman, watching – a mother? a wife? – a presence conceived as he'd listened to Pergolesi's *Stabat Mater*.

John Kani, as Martinus who has killed the white man who'd raped his wife, and Sean Taylor, as Gideon who has fought and killed in South Africa's border wars, are both haunted by their acts. On New Year's Eve Gideon, seeking a "hip-hip-hooray" time at Playland, encounters Martinus and, through a long night, each man descends into his particular hell and eventually extracts the agonizing truth from the other. First light of the new day of 1990 brings no easy reconciliation; but from that truth, from the *listening*, comes a simple, shared determination to break from the prison of the past.

'Warning ignored, prophecy fulfilled,' Athol said of the play. *The Blood Knot* had given the warning – Morrie and Zach, innocents linked by brotherhood, had "come to the brink". Now, after more than thirty years of escalating violence, Martinus and Gideon were strangers linked by each having broken the Sixth Commandment: "Thou shalt not kill."

At the Market Theatre, Sean, in performing before an audience of black teenagers, had felt he was every individual who had ever killed in a war.

❖

Early in 1994 my citizenship and my passport were returned. Gail and John Gerhart were now living in Johannesburg – Gail, teaching and editing a massive history of the struggle, and John, head of the Ford Foundation's work in the region. They settled me in a cottage in their garden.

Athol was in the city, creating a play with five young women, chosen from auditions with high-school students. He had not intended the cast to be all-female but they had shown far greater potential than any of the boys. Busi and Shoki were black, Gamy Asian, Heather white, and Riana of mixed race. He saw it as a chamber quintet for which he would interweave their stories.

On Sundays, over a light lunch in the cottage, he spoke about the production: 'The girls came in as complete strangers to each other. And I thought, this is fascinating, I am being led into the future by five young people and we are going to be able to explore the racial dynamics of South Africa.' His laughter rang out. 'The huge enchanting disappointment is that they came together as a sisterhood. They have learnt from each other – they didn't know about each other's worlds.

'I asked them to keep diaries and acted as amanuensis to them. You have to pick up clues – "No-no-no-no, what do you mean by that?" – and by way of good Socratic dialogue one gets at the truth. It's never abrasive, even what turned out to be our one significant confrontation – a very dramatic confrontation between, on one side the four "Christians", very much of the same culture of young people, discos and so on, and beautiful Gamy who, at sixteen, has such serenity and strength and joy in her Tamil tradition. They asked her, "What do you mean, your mother wants you to marry a Tamil! What if you meet a nice Afrikaner? Or a nice black man?" She just says, "It's my destiny." And they go berserk, "What do you mean, your destiny!" And she quietly stands her ground, not apologetic, not wilted, just tries to explain – the passion with which she tried to get them to understand!

'Her success was measured by something Riana said to me – how important the experience had been for her, since at one level the people where she lives in Eldorado Park regard Indians as "skellums", but also in terms of her religion – "These Indians," she said, "pray to idols, some look like elephants, some like monkeys. But what Gamy has made me realize is that all these gods are different faces of the same God. It's God the protector, the destroyer, the sustainer. What I realize now is that Gamy is praying to God the same way I do."

'I thought, man, this project is worth that statement alone! I've learnt from all of them. And I thought the four girls will sit at the edge of the stage, with Gamy standing right at the back, and they will tell the audience about their confusion, their frustrations about Gamy and then she, speaking over their heads, will have the final word to the audience.'

He spoke of the need to encourage and provoke: Shoki had written about going with a friend to a bar where there were only whites; after ordering beer, they'd wanted a cigarette and a man, middle-aged, sitting nearby had a pack; her friend was too shy to ask so she asked and he said, 'Here you are.' 'End of story!' Athol exclaimed, and went on, 'My questioning drew it out: when they'd entered the bar and realized they were the only blacks, they noticed everybody was staring at them with eyes that said "Who the hell do you think you are?" So they'd invited the man, quite a tough Afrikaner, to join them, and they had a lively conversation including their asking whether he might be a chauvinist, as she certainly was a feminist.'

Athol was continually making discoveries about their lives; the violence. One, beaten and kicked by police, another a witness to her uncle assaulting her aunt, yet another who said that's nothing, to have to watch your sister being raped, that's really dark. A third told of her exercise walk near Witbank in the half-dark of early morning when a black man approached holding something in his arms under his jacket; she didn't like the look in his eyes as he passed; soon after, a police car drew up and two young cops insisted that she get in, it was a dangerous place; they caught up with the man and stopped to ask him for a cigarette and, while he searched, the bundle he was carrying burst open to reveal the arm of a white woman, wearing a gold wristwatch and rings on three fingers.

And they sang – Busi her family's evening songs; Heather's voice, from low notes warming to higher and yet higher, until it shimmered; and Gamy, the chants her family sang early each morning while lighting lamps in their little temple and anointing a Slingaberry tree with milk and tumeric water.

Week after week Athol talked with excitement and affection about these young women who had trusted him with their confidences, their fears and hopes and, as he was leaving the cottage, we looked out on the veld which stretched across the road, on birds flying from telegraph wires to trees shaken by the winds of early autumn. All this at a time of mortal cruelty, of disclosures of the malign activities of a Third Force, killings which for years had been publicized and yet, especially among the Zulus, continued uncontrolled.

'None of their leaders,' said Athol, 'is thinking of South Africa, only of themselves and their lust for power.'

My Life they called the play. With previews imminent, Athol and Mannie, who was producing and lighting it, were still pondering what to do with the final moment. 'Then,' said Athol, 'in conversation with Rebecca, my young assistant, I suddenly realized that she had valued and understood the significance of the young women at levels even I had not really appreciated. And I suggested that instead of another speech about reconciliation which would drive me absolutely mad, what if we could challenge the audience in some way, not crass but in a meaningful way? You write it, I said to Rebecca, and she did!

'The substance was what the group had said in the past, she brought it together. A really beautiful piece for them, anchored round the white girl because she was the one who'd made the biggest journey from ignorance, from innocence, to understanding what the world's about. So Rebecca, using her and bringing the others in, reached the essence – their dignity, their having the courage to be honest with us, the audience: "We've given you our stories, what are you going to do with them? How are you judging us because we know you are judging us." It was very simple but just right; she kept the tone of each of the five voices, each voice with its unique quality.'

Athol invited a few friends to the first "exposure" for the five young actresses: Heather a lissom seventeen-year-old; Riana a bouncy sixteen-year-old; Gamy the quiet Tamil; Shoki so tiny that after she had joined protests at school and been beaten by police, she was made a mascot by comrades, a scene which precipitated their joyous toyi-toying; and Busi whose singing and aerobics energetically opened the play. Riana mimed the start of her days, gazing into a mirror to work out a smile, belting out 'I'm every woman, it's all in me ...' They acted out the first encounters with each other and the conflicts, and they sang and danced.

Then came the ending conceived by Rebecca. Heather silenced our enthusiasm. 'So? What do you think?' she demanded. 'We have given you our hearts...' and she challenged us to imagine lives filled with violence – Shoki, getting caught up in a taxi war and being so badly hurt she had to be taken to hospital – 'I didn't imagine things like that. Well, you try to imagine what would happen to you if you met four strangers in a room and you began to share ... If we are going to build a new country that is what we have to do, isn't it?'

Each in turn took up the challenge, until Riana, full of fun, confronted us: 'What I want to know is do we get a big plus-plus-plus mark or not? ... Because I just know, you were judging our bodies when we were doing aerobics. I know it! So, who's got the best one? Have you decided who's the prettiest? Did you like the way I sing R&B?'

True! In those aerobics I'd studied each one's appearance, and had wondered how Riana of the heaviest legs could kick so high. They had given us their stories; what of us and our lives?

Afterwards, over dinner at Horatio's fish restaurant, a contented Athol remarked, 'I could never have worked out such a production if there'd been boys, what would they have come up with? Locker-room stories? Anecdotes about soccer? Those girls, it was not as if they were playing Joan of Arc – though it's hard just to be on stage, that would have been easier – but to be on stage as themselves!' He hinted that he was already conceiving a play in which he himself would take that risk.

Was there a lot of laughter in their working together, I asked. 'Laughter!' he exploded. 'We died! We died!'

Yvonne Burgess
Pulled In

When they finally pulled him in he needed hospitalization so they put him in a big white bed in which his emaciated frame, little more than skin and bone, hardly tented the sheets. He half sat up against the pillows most of the time, eyes round and wide and staring straight ahead. He must have been in a state of shock or bewilderment or surprise, who knew? Because for the first few days he said nothing. His jaw hung slackly and his mouth, with craggy teeth and vertical overlap, looked like the entrance of a small, dark cave.

And that was the way of it until the nourishment dispensed drop by drop straight into his stringy veins began to take effect and he began to fill out, turning from parchment to pink, his eyes beginning to reflect light and to move, to see, to respond almost intelligently.

They had combed his hair (too long now, wispy and white) with a wet comb, so that the thin strands stuck together and strips of pink skull showed through. They had shaved him as well, but left, at his pitiable pleading, the promise of a moustache. Spiky and white, not quite symmetrical – a little unbalanced, in fact, being noticeably thinner and longer on one side – but a moustache none the less; and besides it was difficult to judge, unless one stood squarely at the bottom of the bed.

So he lay, day after day, tended by large nurses in tight white uniforms which rode up over their extended rumps, and small chirpy nuns, most of them old and frail as their charges, their orders having failed to attract many novices in recent years and they, therefore, a dying breed themselves.

For some time after he'd been pulled in, he had rambled in a feverish, disjointed way about what he called, with a crooked, pained smile, the "brotherhood of the road"; of how he'd been prepared to do anything to survive, old soldier that he was and inured to hardship, but that he'd drawn the line at eating Koksie Harmse's stewed cat and drinking meths diluted with Mix Eleven and water. Rather starve, he'd said.

And so, of course, he very nearly had.

He also rambled on about a number of women: Evadne, Mavis, Anna – sometimes Annie – and a girl, Lillith; but enquiries among the vagrants in the public parks instituted by the welfare services yielded no clues as to their identities – wife, sisters, a daughter? – nor could he enlighten them, disoriented as he still was.

The matter was handed to the police eventually and the Salvation Army and they, fortunately, came up with a few facts: he was Rudyard Kipling Knoesen, one-time inmate of a State work colony, one-time awaiting-trial prisoner, later certified a depressive sociopath and twice detained in a State Mental Hospital at the President's pleasure.

With the link to the State's Mental Health Services thus established, and through the good offices of the Chief Psychiatrist – who may or may not have been pricked in his conscience regarding what may have been a premature discharge from a psychiatric Aftercare Centre – Rudyard Kipling Knoesen was declared an ailing indigent with neither family nor visible means of support, and placed in a Home for the Aged run by the Roman Catholic Church, he having previously designated himself a Roman Catholic, albeit lapsed – an extremely fortuitous circumstance, since, if he had not been pulled in he would undoubtedly have been reduced to eating some of Koksie's concoctions sooner or later.

So here he was in the Home and, from what he had seen so far, in the company of old women who shuffled about in slippers, and a few, a very few, old men like himself, and eating what he later said may not have been cat, but looked and tasted as if it were.

But, of course, he was grateful for having been pulled in. The memory of his many deprivations while on the road (although strictly speaking he had never really been on the road; he had only been in the park) had haunted him until latterly when his memory, mercifully, began to develop large blank patches, becoming like a pool in which images, some recognizable, some not, floated in and out without much reference to conscious thought processes.

He didn't want to remember where he'd been, the cheap hotels, sleeping on broken bedsprings, in Salvation Army hostels and even, one unforgettably humiliating night, in the doorway of a pharmacy.

Best forgotten of course; and so, expedient to the end, and pragmatic as always, he allowed his memory, like his religion, to lapse, recalling unrelated events and people quite arbitrarily; like his friend Annie, the dear girl who had suffered from bipolar emotional disorder. Annie of fond memory, or what was left of it.

But every now and then he would be able to remember things with disconcerting clarity; the connection would be made as neurons vaulted synapses and he would all but taste it again: the sickly sweet Jeripigo, Muscadel, or Hanepoot, with whatever they had added to give it "skop" as Zolah used to say. It could kill, the stuff they drank; it could blind one, cause aneurisms all over the brain, veins popping like balloons as the fumes filled and ruptured them. Not the way he'd ever wanted to go, sodden and senseless.

Suddenly he heard Annie again: 'This isn't the way'.

Damn right, he thought, screwing his eyes up against the pain behind his eyeballs and seeing her as he had seen her last, ethereal in white. She'd never worn white before. Dazzling against her pale skin; white on white, with that flaming mane of hers. Why hadn't she realized how striking she was? And what had she said about resembling the Flanders Mare? Or Anne of Cleves? Anne of my heart, he should have told her. Or maybe he had?

Always putting herself down. Annie, too young and too good for him. Too poor; although she may have stood to inherit ... Too late now, anyway. He struggled to put her out of his mind because thinking about her made the pain worse. Right up into his sinuses now, as if he'd been sniffing fire.

What had crazy Zolah put into the sherry? It had been more than the usual Meths. Ethylalcohol? Surgical spirits? Aftershave? The woman was a misogynist, like all whores. She had a death wish, trying to kill them all ...

Because instead of going with Annie he'd chosen, in his madness, Claude. Claude, like a large crow in his dirty flapping rags, bedraggled and bedevilled. Claude and his cronies: Koksie Harmse and Fatarse or Fartarse (both had been applicable) Froelich, also known as "ou Floors". And Zolah, who'd simply begun to tag along with them, for protection, perhaps; or for the acceptance she could not find anywhere else.

But he'd never really been one of them, he knew that; not the way they eyed him thoughtfully, obviously wondering whether the association could be turned to their advantage in some way, financial preferably. Cash or kind. His jacket hadn't been too bad. Nor his shoes.

He'd have been no match for them and so, when he felt matters coming to a head, he had pointed to his flies and some bushes on the far side of the greenhouse and veered off, away from them, squinting first with one eye then the other, trying to focus, taking a crab-like route because for some reason his right leg had locked at the hip, and was behaving like an oar, forcing him to proceed in circles. He'd had to battle to get away from them, every inch of the way, trying to devise a plan but finding that his brain was in no better shape than his eyes or his leg.

Even now, just remembering started the clamour in his head, a pounding, agonizing conflict as though the right and left sides of his brain had become detached and were rubbing up against each other like tectonic plates, causing seismic shocks and tremors.

A bloody continental drift going on in my head, he thought, expecting his skull to explode at any moment, to erupt, blowing his brains to kingdom come.

He leaned back against the pillows to calm himself and to try to think: first things first. His suitcase. He hadn't sold it, had he? Not that the contents were all that valuable; but the suitcase itself was worth something. It was an antique. A leather relic from bygone days. Nicked from Evadne, when he decamped, before the breakdown. The first breakdown. And maybe it would help, he told himself, to get things in chronological order; maybe it would ease the friction between the plates ...

All right then. He'd had no choice to speak of. It was Claude and the gang, or find himself another Mavis, she of the sweaty, really rank armpits and quivering bosom, the straining silk blouse, cheap brooch and even cheaper perfume.

Or even go back to old Mave herself? Could he bring himself to go into that house again, that large pink pile she'd turned into a boarding-house after the death of her husband, the Captain, with its big pink maw of an entrance hall which swallowed one before Mave began the digesting, the rendering down?

If she would have him back; which she swore she wouldn't. 'Over my dead body,' she'd said. He might have risked it but if it really were over her dead body her kids would have thrown him out in any case.

He remembered her smell again, the sweat with the heavy overlay of floral perfume. Carnation it had been. 'My crook scent,' she'd called it. Maybe she'd fancied herself a bit of a mol, because by all accounts the late Captain had been into several shady deals, one of them resulting in the acquisition of the big pink pile, the shelter, the refuge which she had used as bait to snare him, knowing he had had no other recourse.

Because it had all been too much for him, trying to get his rent together, and something in advance, perhaps, to charm her into letting him back in the interim, as a boarder, nothing more, so help him, only as a boarder ...

Rudy gave an involuntary yelp as a sharp stab of pain in his back nearly tipped him off the bed. Kidneys, probably. Or the thought of ever having to go back to Mavis, or someone like her.

There had probably been more efficient ways to conduct the peripatetic existence he had latterly been obliged to lead, but then, when it came to really being on his uppers, Rudy had always been a novice, a dilletante, simply improvising as he went along, making a virtue of necessity, hoping earnestly that it would all come to an end and that he would once again enter some sort of comfort zone where someone, anyone, would care for him.

And mercifully it was just then that he had been pulled in to a bed in the Home, run, as he had gathered, by the Sisters Mary.

He asked them about his suitcase, his precious suitcase, the one containing his four black notebooks, his mother's slim, badly foxed volume of verse, the photograph by Debenham, the Professor of Tonsorial Artistics' onyx studs and cuff-links and framed accolade (which he'd managed to trace to a neighbourhood junk shop), together with his own meagre effects.

Like a refugee, he thought. My whole long life, everything I am and have, in one nicked leather suitcase.

And yes, they had it, they said. He'd been lying on it when they pulled him in. He smiled. Lying on it. Protecting it with his own life. Perhaps the pain in his back was due to no more than that, a bruise from lying on the suitcase? Maybe he was all right after all. Maybe his kidneys, and even his liver, hadn't quite packed in yet?

When he was finally up and about again, one of the nurses came to take him to his room and he wondered that the place looked so familiar, the long passages intersecting at small lounges; the dining-room, the Matron's and staff offices and restrooms, the dispensary and sickbays, all polished tiles and brass handrails, with doors along either side of the passages.

But then, all institutions were much the same, especially charitable and State institutions; and at least he had his own room, with his own neat little nameplate.

One of the Sisters Mary had come along to see if she'd got the spelling right. She'd written Mr R.K. Knoesen but after Rudy had protested, pouted and sulked for a few hours she'd relented. What did it matter, after all, as long as it made the old man happy? And so there it was: COLONEL R.K. KNOESEN (Rtd).

He had his own little cubicle (calling it a room was a tad hyperbolic), and his own nameplate. He belonged.

At the end of his passage he discovered a small lounge where no one ever sat. It seemed to be used exclusively for funeral teas of which there were many. Not surprising, of course, since everyone there was so old, all living on borrowed time, as they informed him, if threescore and ten were indeed the allotted life-span, or fourscore, by reason of strength.

Only what strength, Rudy wondered. There was nothing to them but nodding heads and endlessly masticating gums, like a flock of ancient sheep ...

At the end of the other wing, and just past the dining-room, was another, bigger sitting-room where most of them did congregate day after day, while those who had arrived too late had to be content with the closed-in verandah where, inexplicably, all the chairs had been placed against the partitions under the windows so that they had to sit facing inward with nothing to look at but rows of linen cupboards.

No one seemed to notice. Too old probably. Especially the women. Old beyond being women, dressed in crimplene and shiny celanese and orlon twinsets. He felt caught in some strange time-warp. It was the forties and fifties all over again. And the sixties, if one took the nurses into account. Tunics above the knees, all of them, even the blacks, although he had heard that it was considered shameful for Xhosa women to expose the backs of their knees.

Not the sort of thing one should be asking about, he didn't think, especially in the new dispensation.

They were a pleasant lot anyway, amply endowed with flesh and voice, passing unintelligible jokes down the length of the passages, together with observations about him, Rudy, and the others; things they found hugely amusing. Not that he minded; it would be laugh or cry, nothing else for it in that place, as he soon saw.

Because that was it: the lounge and passages bristling with walking sticks, wheelchairs and walkers, with old women bent double, hugging their concave or bulbous bosoms; and old nuns in the new skirts just above their burst- and varicose-veined calves, with sandalled feet revealing bunions and corns and other deformities he couldn't even name.

He'd only seen one or two white nurses and they were all on the far side of forty.

Didn't young girls become nurses any more, he wondered? Or didn't the young ones want to work in old-age homes?

Wouldn't his last days have been immeasurably brightened by a bevy of giggling young nurses – student nurses, preferably – with tight little titties and tails, or boobies and bums as they called them these days. Rudy sighed. Fate had always catapulted him into the arms of older women. Older women who had wanted to mother him and since older women tended to be better endowed, at least financially, he had as always taken the line of least resistance.

Little student nurses would be part of his final fantasies, as little ballerinas in tutus just skimming their little round rumps had once been.

Because in that place even the cat was old and sway-backed, lumbering along with its legs out of alignment. Needed a walker or a wheelchair like the old harpies, he thought; although not unkindly, because who was he to criticize, stringy old man that he had become, as weathered as the rest of them, as weak and quavery with his whispery voice and fluttery, prominently veined hands; still on the hoof perhaps, but only just, shuffling along like an old Chinawoman on bound feet.

There were others far worse, though; men and women who looked like the forgotten inmates of a war veteran's hospital, maimed and mutilated, some with one leg, some with half, some with none at all, squatting grotesquely on the base of their truncated bodies. The result of fractures, apparently of diabetes, embolisms, gangrene ... Sexless, their features barely distinguishable under their knitted caps, like aged Noddys, with opaque eyes and drooling mouths, obsessed with the obscure details of their lives, endlessly repeating their tales, reminding him of the ancient mariner (even the women; in fact, especially the women) weatherbeaten, dessicated, salt encrusted (or at least suffering from dreadfully dry skins) peeling like old lumber, warts and wens like barnacles on their bony cheeks and chins.

He listened to their compulsive storytelling without hearing much, his attention span erratic, the stories barely heard, with much that was vital missing (or were they leaving out many of the vital parts?). But he preferred it that way; it made what he did hear so much more curious and evocative.

They'd all lived too long, but were any of them ready to die? What made a man ready to die, Rudy wondered. That was the question. He'd have to consider it, sooner or later, and preferably before he felt the Grim Reaper's foetid breath ... In the meantime, there were the other foetid smells to consider: sourish smells, with an overlay of body odours, urine, even excreta sometimes, rising from the resident's clothes, carried on their breath ...

Of course he, Rudy, wasn't incontinent yet, unlike many of them whose functions, uncontrolled and unselfconscious, caused acrid, nose-twitching smells to emanate from the beds, the chairs, the saturated mattresses and damp upholstery – damage done before the waterproofs could be brought out.

There were other smells too – disinfectants, medications, food ...

Why had he become so conscious of it? Was the olfactory organ in the business of compensating when the other senses began to fail?

They all gave the appearance of being human, walking, talking, eating, sleeping, but they were already on the way to becoming a sub-species, something less than men and women, on their way out ... all but blind, deaf as both jambs of a doorcase ...

But how much of that was genuine? Hadn't they all begun hearing only what they wanted to hear? Wasn't he learning to do that as well?

He had always had one reasonably good ear. The other drum had calcified long ago, the result of ear infections which his mother had treated with warmed sweet oil.

He remembered the occasions well – the sharp stabs of pain, his yells and then the oil poured carefully into a teaspoon blackened underneath from many similar operations, the match lit and the oil warmed before he'd have to lie down on his mother's lap, ailing ear up – the right one usually – for it to be poured in.

Ah well, no blame attached, no recriminations, no hard feelings, even. It was before the advent of antibiotics, after all, when every mother did as she saw fit and as best she could.

He'd surprised himself with the sudden memory of his mother. Perhaps that would be the way of it, then, with nothing too interesting from the outside, he'd be left with the interior life for stimulation, his own reflections and cogitations which he'd always found engrossing enough and perhaps, in that place, in the complete absence of other distractions, he would really be able to think and even express his thoughts again?

He'd ask for paper and a ball-point and get down to it; sometime soon, he promised himself, because, whichever way one looked at it, if he was ever going to produce anything it was now or never, that being in the very nature of things if allotted life-spans were to be taken into account.

Christopher Hope
St Francis in the Veld

The De Tromp family, Tookie and his wife Tina, lived on the farm, Lamentation, out in the Red Hills with their son, little Jamie, who got religious later.

Some said Jamie got religious because his dad got righteous. Others said, yes, no, O.K., but Tookie got righteous, in the wrong way. Not properly righteous like the British Israelites who lived out in Nickleton and said they were descended from the Queen of England.

Tookie got orders to improve the facilities for the wandering folk who rode the donkey carts from farm to farm, pots and pans tied on with baling wire, not a cent in their pockets or food in the bellies of their scraggy kids. Looking for a little shearing in the season; or fencing. They would do anything; they had nothing; they blew every last cent on white wine and dancing and the getting of yet more skinny kids. Never had a roof, a bed, a table; just pulled rusty sheets of corrugated iron from beneath their carts and made a little tent for the night.

Nobody liked them; not farmers, labourers nor town-dwellers. Too rough and ready; so damn reckless it made people want to spit just to see their tracks on the dusty road, two long wandering lines where the cart wheels meandered this way and that through the hot silence. You could have built them palaces, and they'd maybe stay for a while – then one day, out of the blue, the call came ...

'My blood's up,' they would say.

Next morning they'd upped sticks and vanished.

For these people he was told to build outhouses. Flush toilets. Running water. Septic tanks. Monthly collection by Lutherburg Sanitary Services.

'Righteous anger was just welling up in me,' Tookie told Donnie over a beer at the Hunter's Arms.

'Welling?' Donnie frowned.

Tookie nodded. 'Up and up. Like a borehole.'

'Jissus Tookie! Listen brother. Like a volcano, hey! You know why's that?'

Tookie said: 'No, I don't know why's that.' Even though he did.

'It's 'cause the Last Days is coming.'

Donnie was a British Israelite and the Last Days were his big thing. He'd been just another farmer over Scorpionpoint way, strong as a log, big bare legs running like steel cabling out of his tiny shorts all the way down to his thick brown socks. Then one day he got the call, sold up and moved out Nickleton way where the Israelites had their temple. Lived in a little shack. Hung a poster on the back of his bedroom door, ruby branches, glowing like a candelabra. It was the divine family tree of the true Lost Tribe. All the others were fakes. The sacred line of true Israelites ran straight from Adam, in Eden, to Queen Elizabeth in England, to Donnie in Nickleton.

For Donnie everything came down to volcanoes and how hot lava would crisp the planet. In the Last Days everyone was for the high jump. Everyone except the Israelites because their God, Yaweh, was backing them. Without Yaweh they'd be trapped like the rest of the planet.

Donnie was always seeing signs:

'Say you're driving back from Beaufort West. You see a woman hitching – O.K.? Do *not* give her a lift.'

He dropped his voice so that Pascal Le Gros serving doubles in the corner wouldn't hear.

'It's a plot, O.K.?'

'What's a plot?'

'Certain women getting you to sleep with them. They take your sperm prisoner.'

'Why'd they want that?'

'They need your brain power? How else do they get it? That's the plot, O.K.? It's not sperm, as such – right? They're out to grab our genetic codes. Yaweh's warned us, O.K.?'

Donnie was always trying to sell the Israelite angle. The world was overs-cadovers. Join now and be saved.

But Tookie wasn't buying. He bought only what he saw – and he had seen the letter instructing him to erect suitable waterclosets and septic tanks for his itinerant shearers. In its dying days, the old regime had tried to cuddle up to the farm workers. Hoping they'd win a few votes.

Tookie didn't like it but it was in writing and so he did it.

His wife Tina didn't like it either.

She was a little pale, faintly blonde woman with good ankles and broad shoulders and she sat on the sofa in the lounge, beneath the giant gold wristwatch that hung beside the views of the Snow Mountains, talking to Miranda, the doll in her lap. A very clever person was Miranda with big green eyes and skin as smooth as butter.

Tookie's building work was a long way from the farmhouse. But Miranda said if they used the sights on Tookie's hunting rifle this would give them a good view. And, as usual, Miranda was right.

Looking through the telescopic sights Tina watched the towers of grey breezeblocks growing on a patch of veld.

'Dear Heaven, no good will come of this.'

The jam wagon was going to trundle out to Lamentation once a week and pump the stuff out of the septic tanks just like it did in Lutherburg, bringing to the quiet country of the Red Hills the business of the town.

Tina looked down at Miranda: 'Did we marry this man to be touched by the town? Or for the peace and privacy of the far country where people do not visit and each day is peaceful under heaven?'

And Miranda opened her green eyes wide as windows.

Tina asked if Miranda wished the town to come to the farm and Miranda shook her head. She asked Miranda if she wanted the horrid building to stop and for the breezeblocks to come tumbling down – and Miranda clapped her hands. She asked Miranda if she could love someone who fell to building little houses in the veld and Miranda pressed her knees together. She asked what would happen to her poor son, Jamie, when the town came to the farm and Miranda shivered.

To start with anyway, Jamie seemed fine. He had always been a keen little farmer. Driving the tractor when he was just seven, managing the bakkie by ten; a fine shot in the springbok season. A pale little fellow and very quiet and always older than his years, and a hard worker.

Jamie saw the outhouses going up and listened to his mother talking to her doll and he worked even harder. As Tookie's righteous anger welled up in him and he spent more and more time on his project, the day to day business fell to Jamie: he was in charge of dipping the sheep; he began patching the mud wall of the dam against next year's rains – if they ever came; he got the fences fixed.

And he got quieter. Every morning after breakfast he slapped on earphones and was off to the fields, tuned to Radio Salvation – "Your Station for non-stop prayer and rejoicing in the Lord".

Around December time a travelling family arrived in their donkey carts. For Tookie this was D-day. His righteous anger had brought forth the desired result. Three outhouses stood ready. Modern, the best you could build, ceramic cisterns, good chains, real wooden handles: and a sheaf of pages torn from *Farmer's Weekly* strung through a hoop of baling wire on the back of each neat green door.

Tookie directed the new arrivals into the field he'd prepared; he was as excited as a man reversing a brand new harvester into his barn.

The wanderers outspanned their donkeys and tuned their radio to a rock station from Cape Town. That was the thing about them; no money or work or food but always a radio and a scrap of tobacco. There was a thin guy with high cheekbones and narrow eyes who said he was Tom and his wife Klara, who said nothing and looked about fifteen, and three kids: Sticky Thing; Little Nothing and Hippo Girl.

He had no shearing work but Tookie set them to lining his fences with rocks to stop jackals tunneling under the wire and taking his sheep. Tom and Klara toiled in the blazing summer sun, heaving boulders into a hand-cart and pushing them along the wire fence that ran like a knife across the freckled koppies. The travellers camped beside their cart and he saw the glow of their fire of an evening. First thing every morning, last thing at night, he checked out the distant field through the telescopic sight on his hunting rifle.

But when he drove over to take a closer look he got a shock. Tom and Klara had taken the paper from the doors, he told his wife, and used it to light the fire.

Tina said nothing. But Miranda opened her green eyes and piped up that what could someone expect if he played with fire?

But Tookie, he just said: 'Getting used to it takes time.' And he cut more paper. He spent a lot of time pointing his rifle at the horizon that December and wondering what to do.

When the school year ended, Tina and Miranda talked about letting Jamie go to the new school in Lutherburg because the village school was letting in township kids. It wasn't about race or colour, said Tina. No it wasn't, Miranda agreed: it was about keeping up standards. And Jamie's future.

Jamie didn't have much holiday: he worked out in the fields all day, singing along with the hymns on his radio.

'The Lord is My Country/My future and my past/I shall live in Him/First and Last ...'

The nomads fixed the fence. At night their fire blazed and when Tookie went over to the field he found all the fresh paper had vanished from the door.

Tookie got in the bakkie and drove into Lutherburg and bawled out the new town clerk, who had come to office since the Big Change. But the clerk said he was sorry, only it was none of his business what sanitary arrangements people made.

Tookie told Pascal Le Gros over a beer at the Hunter's Arms and

Pascal said: 'So don't replace the paper, O.K.? People got rights. But they also got responsibilities. They got to learn – use it or lose it. that's democratic ...'

But Tookie couldn't do that – it wasn't about politics; it was about doing it properly. He tried even harder. The righteousness was so strong in him he just went on cutting up old *Farmer's Weekly*s, really fast. And just as fast they got burnt. And he even gave Tom and Klara the usual goat for slaughtering on Christmas Eve. And a five litre plastic bag of sweet white wine.

'He's mad!' said Tina.

And Miranda nodded.

On Christmas Day Tookie, Tina, Miranda and Jamie sat down to roast lamb but it was an uncomfortable lunch. Jamie asked if he could say the grace and it went on for about five minutes because of all the people he prayed God to save; besides sinners and adulterers and captains of industry, he prayed also for those who took from the Lord the righteous anger that was His alone and spent it on the base things of the world.

Seated upon Tina's lap, Miranda nodded her approval and glanced at Tookie but he was already wolfing down his food, eager to get back to his rifle and his chair by the window.

He sat there maybe five minutes then he said:

'Come here, man, and take a look-see at this, hey!'

'No, thank you,' said Tina. 'I've got better things to do on Christmas Day than stare at some old Hottentots.'

But Miranda said she would have a quick peep. Tina helped her to squint down the rifle-sight and Miranda squealed. Then Jamie had a look and grew very pale and tuned into Radio Salvation, turned up the volume so loudly Miranda covered her ears, and left the house, saying he was off to dock sheep tails.

Through his rifle-sight Tookie watched the nomad couple circling the remains of their fire and he could see the carcass of the headless roasted goat. Tom and Klara were carrying enamel cups which he felt sure contained the white wine he had bought them. They moved around the fire hand in hand, in a kind of rutting dance, and he knew their radio was blaring out rock music. But the worst thing was that Tom was naked from the waist up and Klara wore nothing at all.

Of their children there was no sign, they had probably been sent to watch the donkeys grazing the veld and now Tom and Klara were busy making more children, bold as brass, on Christmas Day.

Tookie offered the women another look but Miranda buried her face in Tina's bosom.

'There now,' said Tina, 'You've upset her. I hope you're satisfied, Mr Righteous Anger!'

The next morning when Tookie lifted his rifle to his eye he saw nothing.

He drove over to their camp. He found the fire still smouldering, the goat's head lying where they had sawn it off, its eyes bruised and pleading. He knew the story. The call in the blood had come. They had vanished. His feeling of righteous anger was burning more strongly than ever. He was stamping out the remains of their fire when he noticed that pools of water had formed in front of the outhouses, little dirty lakes.

Pushing open a door he found something so awful he had to retreat to his bakkie and sit there for minutes before he had recovered sufficiently to take a closer look, his handkerchief pressed to his nose.

His eyes had not fooled him. Since they had no paper, they had used small round stones. And then they dropped them into the bowl. When one lavatory flooded they had moved to the next. What had he been expecting? They were nomads. They had moved on.

Some people see the light on the road, others hear voices. Tookie's moment of revelation came in the glimpse of a pile of stones in murky water. A revelation so strong he could not but obey it. Otherwise, surely he would have called his workers to clean the things out. But he did not do so.

When the story began to spread farmers said: 'I don't believe it!' and: 'This guy's crazy, O.K.?'

But he did not hear what people said. For after thinking it

through, Tookie removed the stones himself, cleared the blockage, restrung the sheaves of pages and hung them on the back of the doors and, before long, another travelling family was camped in the field. And each time the thing repeated itself; paper into the fire, stones into the bowl – and each time Tookie cleaned it out – not because he liked it, or them, but because he was righteous.

He went further: he began building more outhouses. He tightened his lips and he said to himself: 'Right, then, just you see who gives in first!'

Nor did he stop being righteous even when young Jamie said he wanted to be a weekly boarder in the whites-only school in Lutherburg, because the state school was "the territory of Lucifer", being full of kids from the township who "loved lechery".

Tina and Miranda got Jamie's trunk ready for the new school and they sewed him his costume for Remembrance Day when the boys in waistcoats and the girls in tutus of blue and white and orange danced around a flag pole from which flew the old national flag, and sang the old national anthem.

On the first day of term, Donnie came to the school to warn them about genetic codes and the end of the world, though the headmaster asked particularly that there be no mention of sperm. So Donnie told them instead about the anti-Christ.

'He lives in New York with a lot of Jews and Masons and plans to steal your genetic codes by methods which you will learn when you are a little older.'

Young Jamie lapped it up. He got religious. He began to talk just like Radio Salvation, mixed with the stuff he got from Donnie.

It is pretty unsettling when a twelve-year-old boy tells perfect strangers: 'My ambition is to labour in the Lord's vineyards all the days of my youth. I pray for my people and my culture. My favourite sport is rugby but my favourite occupation is fighting the anti-Christ.'

At weekends he went home to Lamentation where he was more useful than ever with the fences and sheep and the dams because his father was toiling among six new outhouses. Tookie swore that if six could not break his spirit, why then let him build another six, nine, twelve and see what the wanderers would do with those! He wasn't giving up or going under. Let them destroy, Tookie would clean and restore and build anew.

This stuff drove Lutherburgers dippy. What a bloody family! Look at the wife, they said, talking to dolls and the son trying to be a predikant before he's fifteen and the old man building a suburb of outhouses. A slave to his servants. Up to his elbows in it! He embarrassed the hell out of everyone!

Strangers kept bringing it up. Usually visitors lured to Lutherburg by Pascal Le Gros, over at the Hunter's Arms.

'Pilgrims,' he called them. 'People go to Lourdes for miracles, O.K. Why always go after foreign saints? Answer me that. We got our own saint, right here. Let's support him, hey?'

When some folk said – Shame, he should leave Tookie De Tromp alone, Pascal's face purpled up to something past turnip. He hooked his hands under his belly and shifted it with a grunt the way a man lifts a big boulder.

'Why should I hide my light under a bushel, my friends? Bugger that! This is a new country now. We got to reach out to each other. And we need the trade. They come to see the spring flowers – don't they? And the dinosaur footprints. So why not the miracle?'

No ways, said just about everyone. If this is a miracle you can keep it.

Pascal said Lutherburg folk wouldn't know a miracle if it bit them in the bum. He was going after people with a bit of class. Open to natural wonders.

Pascal's pilgrims arrived by coach on Fridays; it was a really good deal. Weekend package, half board. When they got off the bus from Cape Town, pilgrims received a Complimentary Cocktail for the occasion, made by Mike the barman and called Holy Water; white wine, Créme de Menthe, maraschino cherry. The programme laid on was nice and varied: Friday night was karaoke night in the Ladies Bar, followed by Karoo cuisine at its finest; Saturday-visits to the Observatory at Sutherland and the dinosaur footprints; Sunday – Faith in the Veld Excursion.

Before leaving on the Faith in the Veld Excursion pilgrims got a briefing from Pascal: 'Just think you're going to the Vatican. Or mosque or some similar sacred place. So – *respect*, right? Gentlemen, please – no bare feet. Ladies, no shorts. What you will see is the miracle of Lutherburg; a man born to be master waiting humbly on his servants in the veld. The proud man serving the poorest of the poor. A sign of hope. Our St Francis.'

At eleven sharp Mike the barman, in his cherry-red pick-up, led the bus over the dusty roads to Lamentation and parked upwind of the farm. After a picnic lunch and a couple of glasses of wine pilgrims would be led on foot through the veld to within viewing range where Pascal had built a natural hide of reeds.

They would study Tookie through binoculars, slaving among the outhouses, bucket in hand ... In this field, this forest, this cathedral of gray towers, to and fro like a soldier, an army, selfless, unstoppable, moved the saint.

'No photographs, please,' said Mike, the barman.

Afterwards, he took tips.

Peter Wilhelm
The Man Who Had Everything – A Fable

Shortly after the election, Mike O'Riordan found that everything he had taken for granted – including his sense of a place in the world – was swept away. The alteration was really a series of coincidences: one calamity did not follow from another. But in his heart each stage of his dispossession was linked; and in memory there was a seamless flow of disenchantment.

The tides of life had receded: he heard the silence that was left.

In the late summer of that year, when the migrating birds clustered anxiously in the enormous sky, twining together below the final fading remnants of cirrus, he sat in his garden and watched the pool-cleaner tug itself around the great oval of water in which his children had once thrashed in joy. At times the machine heaved itself to the surface and hopelessly sucked at air: a desperate, ineffectual lurch. Twisting and gulping, it sank back into the stainless wateriness scented with chlorine and a remembrance of swooping bodies, clean and young and swollen with life. He saw the cool surface as the skin of drowned memory.

He felt the sadness of lost things. His wife had left him, unable to endure the dark moods and restlessness, the infidelities he took so lightly but that crushed her spirit. And with her had gone the children, down south to a safer city on the sea. In the photographs he kept of them, he saw their eyes big and glossy with knowledge and anticipation as if they too had been yearning to leave, to move out of his shadow. Their remoteness was almost the heaviest blow; how, why had it happened? Perhaps it had happened when he wasn't looking, years ago, when he had allowed his life to become unevenly synchronised with their wishes and wants. So be it.

Even their dog, Gandalf the Afghan, had loped away from O'Riordan, ears down, pushing up into the taxi and settling in the crowded space beneath the departing children's feet. Now he had a cat but the cat was mad; it wandered about the huge house at night howling for company. And in any case, cats did not belong to people: the cat was just a grey presence in his empty, dislocated space. The garden, kept spruce and orderly, extended in all directions like a park until it ran up against the high walls and electric fencing that gave him some form of physical security but which also locked out the world.

He noted the ebb and flow of social change through the intermediation of the television screen; it was neither welcome nor repudiated. More immediate, more real, was the fact that he had lost his work, almost given it away. Even more than the defection of his family – now reconstituted elsewhere with a new husband and father – the worklessness, the state of it, brought the loss of a daily function, of a sense of utility deep in his soul. He was harmed and desolated. It was not that he had no money or had failed at anything: a series of strikes and stayaways at his illustrious chain of food stores had conspired to make the enterprise a lifeless thing for him, and the offer to purchase had come at just that time that he felt the need to sit alone, to think, to start over.

He had not realized how much time would be left. Time and enough to drain his minor loves for golf, music, weightlifting. All lost their savour because there was no work against which to measure their value; it was no longer a reward to listen to Mozart. His mind skidded.

Then there was the loneliness. Where were the others? The friends? What he concluded was that all the friends, lovers and comrades of his generation had emigrated, or moved to another city, or disappeared, or given up. Was it something he had done, or not done? An intrinsic stubbornness kept him in the city – and he loved the flicker of lightning against a stony sky, the breathless sense of vividness the abrupt blaze gave to the stones and walls and windows.

He read books; or sat on the warm slate beside the pool; or walked down to the shops for newspapers and tins of food, a man well past forty to whom no one gave a second glance, wrapped in his secret, trivial story. He stayed in place. The people who mattered, left him there.

Of course he was not truly alone, not in the sense that he had become a casualty – shot dead for his wristwatch or turned socially transparent like some foul overlord from the unjust past. In the house, about the house, at least six servants maintained the momentum of his existence. He scarcely thought about them; he never had before; now they were simply there, neither a good thing nor a bad.

He did not know it, but they gave his emptiness a structure, a container. Without them the walls would have fallen in.

Though his own hold on life was loosening, life did not leave him. When he rose – early as always, as if an invisible alarm had sounded in his mind, a bell – he did what he had never done before: he walked out into the garden, caught and dazzled by the brightness of the day and was struck, hard as a blow between his eyes, by the living breath of creation. The colours of life blazed – cerise bougainvillaea clustered thick on the walls, the green spectrum from gold to ash, the last of night in the silent violet stain that sank below the aching shapes of trees and left the sky clearer and paler in the rush to winter. The colours beat at him; the great chirr of insects and birds that soared made his heart tremble.

Then he would swim, drop like a stone into the cool loveliness of water.

The emptiness came later, over breakfast alone; and later, in the warm cocoon of morning with nothing to do, the newspaper read, his book turned dull; and later, far into the night, when he was restless and unable to sit down or stand up. Cold white wine went warm and stale.

He was ashamed of being workless. It made him feel incomplete and ineffectual. When there had been friends, and they called round, he was morose; and so they stopped calling, stopped introducing him to women.

He drove about the city in his enormous car. The air-conditioning made a sound like unending speech turned low: a cold sibilant caress. The radio stations addressed themselves to momentous issues that fled past him like mercury in tilting dust. He was perfectly indifferent to the idea that there were places where it might be dangerous to go, or that his car could be taken away by violence. If someone in this new, strange city shot him, he considered, that would bring closure: he would slip into the afterlife with grace.

The city unfolded. Where he had worked, managed and inspected, others worked, managed and inspected. From behind the tinted glass of his Mercedes he envied them. He saw, too, the pavements full of work, oranges and lemons, pills and art – all for sale, all stacked and sold and bought. Amid the glittering, abandoned monoliths – tenants scattering north and south to escape engulfment by the unknowable – there were spaces for trade or anarchy in decaying formality, springing into existence in a new formulation of colonialism, green grass in the concrete cracks. There was space and time to sell.

This furious activity – desperate, perhaps, but vivid as lightning – was new to him; he had worked behind blue glass, in a car or an office, within a formal definition of what work meant, what its definition was and how it defined him. He longed to go back to what he had been and done before; the new world seemed to exclude him, for all its expansiveness and promise.

He saw whorehouses where hardware stores had stood. Well: that too was work. The tarts stared enraged after him when he declined. A deep shame suffused him, though not at his indifference to them; in a curious way he wanted to be like them.

The shame was real. He burned. He parked and went to a bar and drank without wanting to, watching the slow movements of those around him, the men who drank before noon in the solace of dim, dying rooms. Drones all, him and them.

He felt old and passed by. The way his body slumped, the way his breath was let out in guarded rations, the shape of his face: he was becoming his father, who had had a poor, bitten life as a railwayman out from Ireland.

Disillusionment had been handed down in the DNA. Yet the way he remembered his father now, it was the eyes glittering in shadow that swam up out of lost time, almost happy because he had once fought in an important war, immeasurably long ago, and ever afterwards each day was both a gift and a downfall from the weight of conflict.

Mike O'Riordan drifted and the servants of his former self tended the vineyards of his lost esteem.

There came a day – no particular one, just another dawn colder than before, winter's edge drawn tighter – when he realized, quite abruptly, that he was wasting whatever remained of his life. It was quite as if a small, still voice, bird-like, had told him so. He had a bowl of porridge before him – placed there for him – and its shape was disturbing: tepid oatmeal that spread out into the bowl and took on its shape. This was the shape of his life.

He couldn't eat; he couldn't go and couldn't stay. Remembering his life as it had been only a year ago was like remembering another's tale, an alluring enough account, but one that was impersonal and distant. Even his children blurred in memory as winter closed its fist. Oddly, only Gandalf the Afghan had distinct features: those trusting eyes and silky nudge!

He felt a profound displacement, and the need for remedy.

Wandering through his abandoned house – abandoned, he knew, by himself – the existence of his servants ceased to be deniable and became overt, stamped on the unusual orderliness of his possessions, the dusted bookshelves and CD cabinet, the straightened carpets, the crumbs swept away and the bed made and hauled taut as a hospital rack. Never in the days of family and labour had his house been so neat and sparkling. And he was quite enclosed in it, sterilized and packed away.

He felt a small anger. Most immediately, he knew, it ought to be directed at himself; but instead he kicked the carpets, spilt his porridge, tugged his bed awry, shifted books around and took a half-glass of whisky and tossed it at the ceiling so the air fumed. Momentarily, he could believe in the servants as machines that scuttled on the fringes of vision and removed the evidence of his presence.

But after he had done all that, the sole sound was the tidal surge of blood in his head. He was left in his shredded-down identity, as he had been before. He needed rearranging, not his earthly possessions — so many that no one had ever known what to give him for Christmas.

In his marginal anguish, he heard laughter. It came from outside the main house, out in the back where the elaborate servants' quarters had been built and turned over for occupation: the place where he never went, from where the servants emerged to scour the house and disappear. Who were they? What were their names? Such matters had always been left for his wife, even payment. Had they been paid at all, once she left? The idea of finding out, of taking on her great, amorphous responsibilities defeated him in advance: the process was too intricate and subtle for comprehension. It was more frightening than a chain of food stores.

Thinking of the energies his wife had commended to her role — her fretful attention to what really kept him afloat — O'Riordan tasted the salt of an unexamined guilt. He phoned. She was down south, far off, safe. 'They've gone swimming,' an unknown voice said. 'Is there a message?'

'Tell them Mike called,' he said. He put the phone down. He had heard his replacement.

Outside, laughter endured. The day was dull. A high wind swept the sky. Each day the sun was lower, weaker. He paced the expanses of his garden, seeing the grass clipped and neat, the flowers stiff in rows, the hedges trimmed. But it all had a depopulated look. The pool-cleaner made tinkling sounds as if it was churning through infinitely thin planes of chiming ice.

He — who had battered his way through life like an iron ship in turbulent seas — approached the place where the servants lived with timidity and discretion. He was not certain why he was going there; the impulse to do so was related to an unassuaged guilt. It was also something to do, a way of making something happen.

His property was so large, and his purse so deep, that there had never been any question of relegating the workers to cramped darkness. They lived in linked cottages, with a communal kitchen and hall; television aerials made indelible spokes against the washed blue sky of winter. And there was a laundry, and garages, and separate entrances, and little rows of beans and tomatoes and lettuces.

And children's toys. He had never known it, but here was a village.

Far more than six people lived here: there was no quick way of reckoning how many, but he saw the forms and structures of families and clan, sprawling and extensive, living space full and vibrant. In his mind the centre of his life shifted from his house – that isolated, cold place – to this fervent hive. Faces lifted to stare at him; the children scuttled; the laughter left and whispers ran. A sturdy woman, fierce and protective, stood before him. He blinked, not angry, not even at himself; but puzzled, inquisitive.

'I don't know you,' he said. 'Who are you?'

'Bessie,' she said, brief and harsh. She knew him. And an old authority, an old respect of hierarchy, brushed them both: but left, drained out of the air like mist in a desert.

One room had been transformed into a repair shop. He saw engines there, stripped and gleaming. He saw people sewing on a bench, making or repairing clothing. Cooking, washing, doing. The impression of a hive intensified. He nodded to Bessie and wandered on, taking it all in. He was amazed. And once they saw his amazement, they turned back to what they were doing, unafraid: not so much ignoring him as dismissing him as a threat, an attitude that was near acceptance but not quite, still infused with a guarded caution. O'Riordan understood that he had a residual power; but equally he understood that they had all seen him in his weakness and solitude and had made their common judgement. There had been a reversal:

he was allowed to linger, there was little more to it than that.

Bessie was behind him. He turned to her. 'You'll need more space,' he said. *And I'll need less*, he thought.

Mike O'Riordan's house lay behind high walls. They were far too high to see over, and the entrance had a shuttered look, chained up against the world. In time the paint faded and peeled; the locks rusted and were left off; the vast gardens were turned over to vegetables and the house itself teemed.

Attracted by the outer evidence of decay, intruders saw the vibrancy of occupation and swiftly left. Some who were not intruders, particularly lost children, were welcomed and stayed.

Years passed.

If, say, you delivered post, you might catch a glimpse of the grounds and the unravelling house: of the space that had taken on the look of a farm, a small, cunning acreage of planting and what could almost be pasturage in the suburban fastness. There were animals there, too, cattle and goats and such. Chickens. It all had a deceptive, rundown look, since the postman, or whoever, if he looked more closely, would see the nets of work and communication, hear the laughter lapping from within against the walls; and in time the walls themselves would go, fall down or be appropriated and supplanted by the new, shining green. And then there were many visitors, so in any case the walls no longer protected or shielded but simply stood there, perhaps a memorial for something which had happened so long ago that the reason for the sagging brickwork, nested within a great entangled bloom of bougainvillaea, had been forgotten.

You might have seen O'Riordan, too, shirt off, digging in the earth. He had his own patch near the vast girth of a jacaranda tree where a grey cat chased bright, lingering birds. He worked through the repetition of the seasons, even in the heat when the purple blossoms fell and covered him with their soft, slow pressure; even in the cold when the earth turned hard and had to be broken up, turned over and levelled; even when it was neither hot nor cold and his mind was distant and he might have been thinking of his wife and children and

Gandalf the Afghan, far from him, at the sea, at play in the bright sun of the beach where the bitter waves slid among the stones.

He worked steadily, that was all. He never cried out for them to come back.

Ahmed Essop
The Banquet

Soon after the Apartheid era terminated and the new era was inaugurated with the establishment of parliamentary democracy, Mr Khamsin, the affluent Fordsburg merchant, bought a mansion in the former élite white suburb of Houghton. Several members of parliament and cabinet ministers had already moved to the suburb when negotiations began with the white aristocracy. The President had also purchased a mansion there, but his manifold official duties demanded that he occupy state residences, and he seldom came to the suburb where his mansion was always kept in readiness for his arrival.

Mr Khamsin's mansion was one of the largest, with wide stretches of lawn in front of a porch embellished with two columns. At the back was a garden with all varieties of shrubs and a swimming-pool. There had been statues of Greek deities, among them that of Apollo, along the driveway and water nymphs near the pool, but the merchant had these removed and sold to an antique dealer as their presence did not accord with religious taboo. Here he brought his new wife, his third. She was a woman in her forties who wore expensive Benares silk saris instead of Muslim garments.

Mr Khamsin soon discovered who the members of parliament were in his suburb and who were men of influence. He called on them in his black Daimler Sovereign. They were pleased to meet him as he was of their social standing. He invited them to a banquet at his home to celebrate the new political era.

It was a full-moon evening when the guests arrived in Mercedes

Benzes and were ushered by attendants into the reception room where a warm welcome awaited them. They were served various kinds of drinks by women dressed in costumes displaying the colours of the national flag: blue, red and green. The host couple moved among the guests and spoke of the new South Africa. Among the guests was Mr Shareef Suhail, a tall man in a black robe and white turban, a small beard and an elegant moustache. There was also an African-American Mr Hunter, with dense ashen hair. Mr Khamsin had met him at a luncheon of business executives in the city and invited him to the banquet.

'All hopes are on you,' Mr Khamsin said to Mr Delani, the Minister of Finance, 'to lift this country to prosperity after the nightmare of Apartheid.'

'Of course, we are all optimistic.'

'I would add confident, for the best men have been appointed to positions in government.'

Mr Delani, a short fat man answered with a triumphant smile, 'Well, we won the elections decisively.'

'After hundreds of years of oppression you deserve your position,' Mr Hunter said.

Mr Delani and his wife had left the country twenty-five years earlier and on their return were hailed as liberators.

'Dinner is served,' a waiter announced and everyone moved to the dining-room.

Mr Khamsin, a fairly tall man with greying hair, his overnourished body enclosed in a dark-blue suit, asked Mr Delani to sit beside him and the Minister's wife next to the hostess. Mr Khamsin made the following speech to his guests:

'Ladies and gentleman, I welcome you all. It is a great pleasure to have you here to celebrate the greatest event in the history of this country, its change from a dictatorship to a democracy that will bring the golden age of prosperity. Democracy is the most priceless pearl in this world. It gives everyone the right to vote for the best people to govern, provides freedom from oppression, guarantees the ordinary citizen justice and equity, and gives him the opportunity to rise to the heavens. In fact I can say that democracy began in Africa from the earliest times. Every subject had the right to talk to his chief or king. This we could not do with the white government, even on trivial matters. You all know how the suburb of Pageview-Vrededorp was brutally destroyed and how our black brothers were banished to homelands. Now, happily, all that is over. Ladies and gentleman, please enjoy the modest fare provided.'

Everyone enjoyed the seven-course meal and after coffee and dainties Mr Delani asked the host if he could say a few words. Mr Khamsin consented and introduced the Minister.

'Ladies and gentleman,' he began, 'our host has spoken of the rise of democracy in Africa. I wish to add to what he has said. What we blacks have been fighting for since we were born is Afro-democracy. It is unlike any other in the world, whether American or European. It is unique, non-racist, non-sexist and non-sectarian. Afro-democracy will see the rise of the ordinary citizen to the height of power. At present, because of circumstances, we have proportional representation, but after five years we shall have a fully elected Afro-democratic parliament which will carry out the wishes of the people. I am sure their main demand will be Afro-prosperity.'

There was applause, led by Mr Khamsin.

After dinner, the guests moved to the lounges, and indulged in conversation.

'I am very interested,' Dr de Jager, a former lecturer in politics, said to Mr Delani and a group that included Mr Suhail, 'in the concept of Afro-democracy. There is no point in imposing a European or American system here. Democracy must be Africanised; by that I mean accepting local tradition and culture patterns.'

'I don't mean exactly that by Afro-democracy. It is more complex and wide-ranging than simply including traditions. Afro-democracy is a viable entity that absorbs all past and future democratic principles. I hope you understand what I mean.'

'Yes,' Mr Khamsin said. 'Our President has spoken of our rainbow nation the like of which is not to be found anywhere in the world.'

'Precisely,' Mr Delani said, 'that is part of Afro-democracy, but not the complete part.'

'What else is there?' Shareef inquired.

The Minister ignored the question.

'Can I venture an explanation,' Mr Hunter offered. 'I am sure Afro-democracy will lead to a restoration of black identity and black dignity.'

'All that and more,' Mr Delani replied with an inscrutable look.

'What more is there?' Shareef inquired again, but the Minister ignored him and turned to Mr Khamsin, 'Can we go outside for a while?'

'Of course. Gentlemen, let us go to the patio overlooking the swimming-pool. We can continue the discussion there.'

They went out and sat in armchairs. Waiters came with trays of delicacies and fruit drinks and bowls containing varieties of nuts.

'In pre-colonial times,' Mr Roden said, 'all land belonged to the people. It should now be returned to them.'

'Why do you exclude mining, industries and monopolies?' Shareef asked.

'Because the land was stolen. That is a fact of history.'

'I am in agreement with Mr Roden,' Mr Khamsin came in, 'though in a modern free-market state all land should belong to those who have agricultural expertise. Otherwise what happened in Russia will happen here.'

'Everyone knows,' Mr Roden went on, 'that the Soviet Union collapsed because the men who ruled were not communists.'

Mr Roden had spent many years in exile in Moscow as a guest of the government.

'With the Soviet bureaucrats communist ideology collapsed as well,' Shareef reminded him.

'We need not debate that,' Dr Farid, a former lecturer in law in London, interposed. 'Let us concern ourselves with the present dispensation. We all agree that Apartheid was a monster. We are now part of a rainbow nation that will set an example to the world with Afro-democracy.'

'Well said,' Mr Delani concurred. 'Capitalism, communism, Euro-cultures have all failed.'

'Euro-cultures, yes,' Mr Hunter took up the theme, 'have not only failed but perpetuated racism throughout the world. Come to America and you will see how racism operates in a Western democracy.'

'Our democracy,' Mr Mohamed (a former legal advisor to Gool, the "protector" of merchants in Fordsburg) said, 'must take into account the legal and political traditions of Africa destroyed by the white colonialists.'

'Not only that,' Professor Ramota, a former lecturer in sociology, spoke for the first time, 'but South africa must shed its Euro-ethos. For a new nation to survive a common identity is essential. Whites have admired Oriental cultures but not African which they labelled primitive. It is now time to demand respect for what is truly African.'

'We need to look at the history written by colonialists and resurrect the rich store of myths and legends, poetry and songs,' Shareef contributed.

'That is secondary,' Professor Ramota continued. 'I am speaking of what is essentially African, that gives us a common identity with all Africa. There is our traditional friendliness, hospitality, consensus in decision-making, the emphasis on the community rather than the individual, the emotional bond with nature, our respect for the aged and our ancestral religion.'

Shareef wanted to inquire if the English language, which was part of the Euro-ethos, should be abandoned, but decided not to.

'There is much more,' Mr Hunter said. 'Africans built the pyramids, they invented hieroglyphics. They were the first prophets. Moses was an Ethiopian. Muhammad had black ancestry. Even the Buddha. I have examined his statues in the East. They have distinct negroid features.'

'If you had examined some of the statues of the Buddha after Alexander's entry into India you would have concluded that he was a Greek,' Shareef said to him.

'In any case, Egyptians, who were the first mathematicians, were all black.'

'Even Rameses II and his queen Nefertari?'

'Even them. Even Cleopatra.'

'Should we not rather speak of the cultural achievements of Homo sapiens in Africa, in Europe, in Asia,' Shareef suggested.

'No. That would deny our specific African identity. Europeans and American whites are racist oppressors.'

Professor Ramota smiled at Mr Hunter. 'You have said what I wanted to say. We have achieved great things. Scientists say that man originated in Africa. Imagine, Adam and Eve were black! We will show the whites what democracy, which is our heritage, really means. They have denied it to us for hundreds of years. We will now offer it to them.'

'Precisely,' Mr Khamsin asserted. 'Modern society is open. There are no hidden agendas. Look at the American Presidential elections. Everything is in the democratic market place.'

'It is a carnival,' Shareef commented.

'A racist carnival,' the African-American stressed.

'Our great President,' Dr Farid extended the discussion, 'is on record as saying that our rainbow nation will show the world that different races can live together in harmony. Oppression, injustice, corruption, genocide, will not take root here. He has even offered to solve the problems of Ireland. He is the greatest statesman in the world today.'

'Thousands of people have died in the Kingdom of KwaZulu because of political rivalry,' Shareef reminded him. No one spoke for a while. Then he added, 'The wisdom of silence is difficult to attain, even in prison.' With this cryptic remark he rose from his chair and said, 'Gentleman, please excuse me. It is a lovely night. I will take a walk in the garden.' He went down the stone steps to the swimming-pool and then disappeared in a nearby shrubbery.

'He is a strange man,' Mr Khansim informed his guests. 'He is a bachelor. He lives in a flat in Fordsburg and drives an old car. I understand he has been appointed as a member of parliament because he spent a few years on the island for his political writings.'

'Exiles have done much to liberate this country,' Mr Delani said while eating pistachio nuts, 'and so have some who remained here.'

'Shareef Suhail has an independent mind,' Dr de Jager offered.

'Such men are dangerous,' Mr Khamsin warned.

'You don't believe,' Dr de Jager asked, 'that thinkers are necessary to the state? I am told he is a historian, a literacy critic and a philosopher.'

'Yes, thinkers like us. Traitors are noted for their independent minds. What we need are men with visions that can be implemented, not men with narrow views.'

'Narrow views?' Mr Delani inquired.

'Some people say he is a fundamentalist. Observe his clothing.'

At this moment they saw Shareef emerge from the shrubbery and walk towards the pool. He stood on the tiled edge contemplating the moonlighted surface.

'There he is,' Mr Khamsin said. 'Come, Mr Delani, let us go and speak to him why he walks alone.'

The two men went down the steps and approached Shareef.

'I have noticed you are keeping to yourself,' Mr Khamsin addressed him.

'Please forgive me. It is such a beautiful night and I could not resist the temptation of walking in your lovely garden.'

'Thank you, but as a distinguished member of parliament you are best appreciated in society.'

'Of course. But a little solitude contemplating nature is necessary for the spirit.'

'You should,' Mr Delani advised, 'go out into the country and appreciate Africa now that it is ours.'

'This is Africa,' Shareef reminded him with a smile.

'Yes,' Mr Delani laughed. 'Houghton is in Africa. We have taken over.'

'Come,' Mr Khamsin said to the Minister, placing his hand around his shoulder. 'Let us also take a walk and appreciate nature.'

'Mr Delani,' Mr Khamsin said as they walked along a gravel path, 'can this country afford to have men like Mr Suhail? Fundamentalists are sowing terror all over the civilised world.'

'I will have to look into the matter.'

'Thank you. I am prepared to serve this country to achieve Afro-democracy and prosperity. If a member of parliament decides to resign or becomes ill ...'

'I will keep you in mind. For the next five years this country needs the best men, men like you. You prospered in spite of Apartheid. I admire you.'

After several months Mr Khamsin was called to parliament when a seat became vacant. Shareef Suhail resigned soon after the merchant's appointment.

Stephen Gray
A True Romance

They took the more private back route up in the lift. Other shoppers were ascending and descending on the escalators, cool out of the summer. They used the opportunity to peck one another: Johan's lips chapped with the sun, John's smeared with Vaseline Lip-Ice.

'Putting KY on your lips now?' Johan said.

John just clenched his hand around Johan's wrist.

The trouble with Johan was he liked to exhibit himself; John preferred remaining furtive. The lift-door opened.

John was taking Johan to be tested. Not his blood or his lungs, but his big blue eyes. Johan avoided reading small-print nowadays, probably because he was less and less able. His struggle with map-reading in the car was making this apparent. His chin rested on the device, a beam lighting up his beautiful eye.

'Glaucoma,' said the optometrist.

'But he's only twenty-two,' said John.

Johan gave a massive blink.

'Just screening – it's mandatory by law.'

'Oh,' said John.

'Well, I haven't got glau-co-ma either,' said Johan.

'That's to be thankful for.'

At first, with the glasses on, Johan walked as if his legs had shrunk. On the down escalator he gripped the moving rail. Outside in the sunlight the glasses clouded over in a satisfactory manner. Johan took them off to study his double mirror image, stuck them back on cautiously with both hands. A whole new, less active, way of life. Now he could read the map, just for pleasure this time ... and the bright route streaming past. 'Check that, just check that!'

At the clothing shop he left the glasses behind in their slipcase on the counter. They had to go back. With the glasses on again, he could examine the weave, the stitching in the seams of his new jeans. He squeezed John's knee as John pressed the buzzer for the automatic gate.

Johan, as it were, tripped up the stairs to John's flat where they had lived together for almost a year. They were still in that preliminary stage of a romance, deeply uncertain of one another. Johan would disappear for days, weeks on end. When he returned, John insisted he be contrite. John had to keep the steady job, mark all those tests, earn to provide – for Johan. In a desultory, undeclared way, they were indeed in love with one another, but the kind of social barriers for which South Africa is famous kept them from settling down as an economical unit too soon.

'*I'll* cook this time,' Johan insisted. Which meant scrambled eggs.

He actually peered into the pan. 'Crumbs, look how – look how it's – clotting,' he said. 'Forming clots.'

No instrument could measure the *extent* of their love-relationship, but for both John and Johan it had grown, let us say, in spite of themselves. John had previously been straight and married, so that this was his first gay affair and all that entailed. Johan had hustled since his teens, lived with a few older men of some status until the thieving departure; mostly one-night stands to keep off the streets. This unlikely liaison with dour John was a big event for him, as well.

In bed they were learning to achieve closeness, sometimes frighteningly so. With less alcohol, and earlier at night, they now could spend hours on each other, at the nooks and crannies of bodies that had not been really alert to others before. Occasional ecstasies, but nothing like this engrossment. They were learning to express themselves more through themselves. That is why the stolen buss in the lift was not so much a surprise as a proclamation to themselves that they actually did care for one another.

As they were both in their own ways Puritan (Johan – low class Afrikaans, John – residual Presbyterian stock) and thus not much trained to treat others with delicacy, it had crept up on them: love was now wishing the other greater fortune than one wished for oneself. Clingingly, they had both become so *considerate*.

Given their personal histories, this was all the more remarkable. Johan's was obvious, indeed written on his lissome, creamy body: the chink where his baby head was bashed into a table, leaving a ridge beneath his right eyebrow; the scars which were more than accidents – stripes on his buttocks from reformatory life; also two strokes of the razor-blade at the left inside wrist. Yet he was always undressing as if others could not read the signs, holding his balls, focusing on himself in the mirror. *Needing attention.*

John, twice his age, had every reason to stay covered up. Old freckles lately were turning into eczema. Johan was too tactful to comment on these; all he would say in the bath was, 'Now I'll really descale – descale your back.' John was too light-skinned to tan without burning. In the complex's dazzling pool, Johan would dive in and glide down the tiles. Horseplay was out because, if John got his head wet, he would go deaf for hours.

It was on the tip of John's tongue to say the words – *do you love me?* Just over a salad on the balcony, without a change of register. As if they had no more importance than *are you getting used to your glasses now?* But behind that was a larger question: *what difference does it make?*

And behind that: *is it possible for two men to love one another, anyway?*

They had mothers in common.

Johan was trained to the phone ringing on Sunday morning, picking it up, passing it over to John without the slightest evidence of his presence if it was John's mother. 'Yes, mother ... yes, mum ...' John would reach around the table for *his* glasses. As if he was undressed without them.

Sometimes Johan just dozed on; sometimes to be really objectionable he would take a piece of John's body – a big toe, or the elbow curved upwards – and work on it during an interminable duty-chat.

Occasionally the wife phoned, but at more considerate times: brisk, reasonable. In fact, although she did have her regrets, she thought it quite intriguing that her husband – inevitably she had found out – had undergone what she vaguely thought of as a sex-change. Obviously neither women had yet met this Johan.

For his part, Johan's mother – to whom he escaped periodically down in Port Elizabeth – had been recruited into the Witnesses. When she was not ill, as her son had formerly, she spent her time on the pavements soliciting – in her case for Jehovah. Jehovah was the best bet for anyone connected to a homosexual case, like that of her own son.

From time to time she wrote desperate notes to him at the post office box they now shared. John would bundle Johan's kitbag on to the Greyhound Bus and they would squeeze hands – just that – at the last possible moment before departure.

And Johan would call with his phonecard from Colesberg, saying they'd got off for supper, and from the terminus to say he'd arrived, his phonecard running out. He would not call again for a whole week. That was how it went: he needed to revert to that other life to which John would never have access, for a while. Just to help him decide.

Then Johan's mother died, too suddenly for her son to be at her deathbed – Greyhound, phonecard, a staggering sum for the funeral, which John provided. For a month after his return from the peculiar wake, Johan was in an unrecognizable state; true distress, even derangement, over the fact that so little had come of his past. He gave out confused utterances, like 'They tell me Jesus doesn't – doesn't drink' – this, falling over the empties in the kitchen.

'Evidently you now do,' said John, which was vindictive. Johan had inherited the working class manner of dramatizing his sorrow.

Then he'd kneel on the Tabriz. 'I'm gonna – I'm gonna –' he'd blink. 'Get her a fucking tombstone –' Which was pointless, since her sour bones had been cremated.

Contrite, Johan passed out, there on the carpet. John had to drag him through, undress him, wash him and smuggle his drooping weight undercover for the rest of the night. Protect him against himself.

John had his crisis, too, one night when he had eaten a Knysna oyster that had absorbed some red tide. Johan, who couldn't yet drive, actually persuaded their general practitioner to make a housecall at two a.m., stomach-pump the victim, inject him and generally save him for posterity. The doctor, having separately attended to their venereal problems, and thus knowing more about the involvements of the pair than they did, simply told Johan: *don't leave his side*. He didn't.

That seemed to be the domestic part of loving: nursing the utterly helpless. Being around to relay to the partner what happened when he was knocked out.

After a long, agonizing commotion John was retrenched from his job. Unexpected new South African factors caused this. Like most of his kind, John had previously lived impervious to anything within touching distance of what may be termed the strictly political. Indeed, the great watershed crossing of the country from apartheid to democracy had occurred smoothly enough, for his taste. In fact, it was the best time to turn out gay: now in South Africa, incredibly enough, he *could not* be discriminated against in the workplace as such.

Nevertheless, he was still a middle-aged white, so that a counter current of affirmative action saw to it that he was replaced, by a rather dopy-looking trainee from Giyani, as it happens, brown as toast and aged all of twenty. Simply put, the new headmaster no longer wanted a stalwart who always got his marksheets in early and commanded such a high salary. John was out, as of the end of the month.

At first all John and Johan could come up with was selling off the former's CD collection. Cutbacks would certainly have to be made. Johan could always go out and get a job — as a welder, the profession he had perforce been taught.

After what in a straight household would be called a bout of marital abuse, triggered by John's despair and resulting in Johan with a lip swollen as if a bee had stung him ... the whole debacle blew over. John got a job in the CD supermarket run by his distant cousin, classical section, nine to five, Monday through Saturday. Johan meanwhile continued to make metal gadgets for the kitchen, which they began to sell together at the local fleamarket on Sundays. Months went by in this way, even years.

John's mother seems to have rationalized the situation of her son. So he had a kind of handyman subletting a room in his flat, paying his way, even taking his shift at the stove as hardened bachelors sometimes could do. When her daughter-in-law informed her, no, they were *screwing* one another, she genuinely had no idea what was meant. She thought it had something to do with those ingenious appliances.

John's gawky young boy was the one to normalize the family network. He would charge into the flat on the days they were due to look after him, literally throw himself at Johan: splat! I do love you, *uncle!*

Johan was looking his best these days: filled-out but still rangy, blond hair like a handful of pick-up sticks, those devastating eyes behind the clear glasses he had taken to. As a salesman of his work, with his vastly improved English, he had developed an easygoing, appealing manner. From the stall he could readily pick up younger men. Steering them to the chimney stack on the roof of the parking garage, he initiated them in turn into certain procedures. The difference from the days of his own street-life was that now he was the one to be doing the blowing.

John of course could tell, by a certain lightness of step on Johan's part, what was up, when, if not exactly with whom, though sometimes he saw the suspects slinking off, the telltale speck on their shorts. To assert his right to revenge, once John took off in the car without explanation, and did not return *until dawn*. Months later, when tricked into it by Johan, he did admit that he had merely stayed in the car, staring at Zoo Lake until the sunrise.

And had tears been running down his cheeks? Yes, buckets full of tears had been coursing down.

It was not yet Johan's turn to cry buckets. That would come after he brought to the flat the degenerate, stoked-up number who, with great dexterity and even violence, insisted on having them both more or less simultaneously. After they paid him off, Johan sank into his armchair and, for no reason whatsoever, simply burst out. They became more faithful to one another thereafter.

When John's three-week annual leave came round, his wife would give them Little John for a while, so the three Johns took off on a carefully planned trip. Once this was fishing on the Transkei coast, at some remote spot where they had to camp, living off nature's bounty. In Little John's case there was no question that affection was a greater tug than biology. He and Johan were perpetually fastened together, prying off bait, getting a licence to harvest their mussels (which John would not eat), building up the driftwood fire. Men at work.

Little John had opted to learn some Xhosa at school, so that when their tent was surrounded by curious herdboys a kind of verbal barter ensued, puffed-up Little John taking the lead. Something he came out with had a dozen Transkeians on their backs in the sand with laughter, responding with a chorus of lurid insults. Johan said they were calling one another "stupid fat cow" and other imbecilities. When John saw Little John doubled up with mirth, then swaggering into a bout of even worse invective, he felt envious: it would be a happier country, giggling.

On their return the father of staunch Little John found himself with the mother. For the first time in over half a decade they were alone together, a circumstance he had avoided; indeed, with Johan as a shield, had prevented.

What made John awkward was her likableness: she was well-together, so amenable. She now saw her husband (they had not bothered to divorce), if it may be put this way, as fully developed at last. He had quit the CD shop, taking a lesser salary as a music announcer on the new radio, finding the way to put over exactly the right mix of his knowledge and of his enthusiasm. She had not thought he had that kind of assurance in him. The greying temples helped. He was not meant to be young any more, and how comfortable he had become in his slack body.

'The programme's going well, isn't it?' she said uncomplicatedly.

'I'm glad you enjoy it,' he replied.

Then she said: 'John ...'

That was all. They were back in their old bed again. They forgot about Little John and the uniforms Johan was buying with him; they forgot, if that's possible, about the difficult intervening years. For her the experience was shattering, scrambled her poise; for him, although his body recognized the old rhythms and performed well, he was no longer inside it at all, but hovering around rather, wondering why he was thus engaged, down there, beside himself. They were grateful to one another, touched ... never were going to try it again. In due course they did divorce quite amicably.

Johan benefited. Towards him John displayed a new kind of tenderness, a sort of feminine grace which at last he allowed to emerge. They'd scream like school-girls, letting it all out. Furious bouts of work on "the programme" followed. Johan shifted his shielding activities to the phone: hopeless fans, late at night, wanting the master's voice (all women, much mistaken). He unplugged it when they were in bed together.

Johan was appointed to run a metal sculpture workshop for some foundation past Sandton. This meant driving lessons and a second car and all that entails. They could have gone on in that style: a cosy twosome, private as all such arrangements are in the bourgeois world, based on a real dedication to looking after one another that neither of them had thought possible. Habit certainly cemented them, but more basically each knew the other could still deliver surprises: thus, fascination.

In the outside world they were separately thought of as accomplished. Without any planning that way, they both now performed social functions which may perhaps be considered nation-building: John in education again, Johan out there with the avant-garde. It was part of the fresh climate.

Their true romance would have continued had Johan not been killed in a perfectly ordinary car-crash at the intersection of Bompas Road and Oxford Road when one afternoon he was a bit late for a session at the workshop. What made it worse was that *he* was in the wrong: he had disregarded the traffic light. Not only was he dead, but due to lack of insurance both wrecks had to be paid for by John. It was all unexpected and unwanted. The man whom Johan hit head-on was unhurt; he could not have been more apologetic. Why hadn't Johan seen him coming?

John went straight from the mortuary to a concert in the City Hall. Every time the light was on beside his mike, he spoke unwaveringly, a true professional. Once he'd returned the listeners to the studio ... his body began to shake. In a sense, it continued to shake uncertainly for ever after. He had had the love of this life; would not have another.

Their experience of this love had been different. For Johan, John had been the *whole* of his life; they had met before he had found himself, and he died while they were still in progress. Even Little John – and his grief was terrible to watch – was experiencing more nuance to his life: a blank, a Johan period and then after-Johan.

So John had now had two lives. Not being as resilient as his offspring (whom he often wondered about – how he was turning out in terms of sexual orientation, had his passion for Johan contaminated him?), he couldn't forget the ghastly accident that easily. The loss stayed with him and haunted him. Often, in the depths of his being, he felt he wished he had been taken instead. That was the extreme of his feeling of love.

They held a memorial service for Johan at the sculpture place, where he was evidently much missed. This was in the courtyard in which a huge work of his, welded together out of industrial scrap, was incomplete. John's ex-wife and son attended, but not his mother (who always knew her son's lodger should never have driven).

Under a jacaranda tree dropping down purple blossoms, the service took its course. They held hands a lot – a very mixed group, some black schoolchildren, housewives, Indians, woodworkers from next door, staff. They sang the first two verses of a heartening hymn.

The clergyman, shaking hands, said he was sorry about John losing his son ... 'No, there he is,' John replied, pointing out the handsome teenager. The clergyman and he realized what had happened and cringed.

John touched the surface of the statue the late Johan had been building. The spot-welds, sandpapered over, reminded him of the scars on Johan's body. The healing process that left traces of the damage done.

John moved to a smaller flat. All there was left of Johan in the end were a few holiday snaps, framed above the music console.

But one night, in spite of the new location – even the new bed – the ghost of Johan found him out. John had the impression the door from the bathroom was slightly opened. Presently there was the weight of hands and knees on the counterpane, trying to crawl between the sheets without waking him. Then the cool back edged into position against his chest, ready for the arms to enclose it and the late-night blurt: 'Love – love you.'

He got up to see if a prowler hadn't broken in. There was no one. But Johan had been there. Of that he was certain.

It was another delayed reaction; his way of saying farewell. That is where their romance, as such, ended.

Ingrid de Kok
Three Poems

Transfer

All the family dogs are dead.
A borrowed one, its displaced hip
at an angle to its purebred head,
bays at a siren's emergency climb
whining from the motorway.
Seven strangers now have keys
to the padlock on the gate,
where, instead of lights, a mimosa tree
burns its golden blurred bee-fur
to lead you to the door.

'So many leaves, too many trees'
says the gardener who weekly
salvages an ordered edge;
raking round the rusted rotary hoe
left standing where my uncle last
cranked it hard to clear a space
between the trees, peach orchard,
nectarine and plum, to prove
that he at least could move
the future's rankness to another place.

Forty years ago the house was built
to hold private unhappiness intact,
safe against mobile molecular growths

of city, developers and blacks.
Now rhubarb spurs grow wild and sour;
the mulberries, the ducks and bantams gone.
In the fishpond's sage-green soup
its fraying goldfish decompose the sun,
wax-white lilies float upon the rot.
And leaves in random piles are burning.

Townhouses circle the inheritance.
The fire station and franchised inn
keep neighbourhood watch over its fate.
The municipality leers over the gate,
complains of dispossession and neglect,
dark tenants and the broken fence.
But all the highveld birds are here,
weighing their metronomic blossoms
upon the branches in the winter air.
And the exiles are returning.

Ground Wave

Just below the cottage door
our moraine stairway of lemon trees,
strelitzia quills and oleander shrub
steps to the sea and deeper terraces.
The warming wind, concertina on the slope,
coaxes open the bulbul's throat,
the figtree's testicular green globes
and camelia's white evening flux.

Behind the house we feel
the mountain's friction against our backs.
Deep fissures are predicted by the almanac,
earth and trees heaving to the shore.
Scorpions come in at night
for cool killings on the flagstone floor.

At the commission

In the retelling
no one remembers
whether he was carrying a grenade
or if his pent up body
exploded on contact with
horrors to come.

Would it matter to know
the detail called truth
since, fast forwarded,
the ending is the same,
over and over?

The questions, however intended,
all lead away from him
alone there, running for his life.

Mongane Wally Serote
Martha, Martha What's Your Boy's Name?

Martha's baby arrived into the world, with a big cry, on a dirty bed, with bloody sheets, in a noisy cubicle of screaming children, women, and a man crying outside in the dark. Martha felt very tired. She wanted water, but the nurse wasn't there to give it to her; she had not been there to see the small boy, Mandela, come. Martha was very happy that her boy had come, and that maybe tomorrow she would go back to her mother with the baby. Nothing mattered now. All she wanted was water and to wait for daylight to come so that she could go home. She heard the yelling children and a moaning woman, and the crying man and the nurses cursing and shouting. But that did not matter.

'What are you doing?' the nurse asked her.

'My baby came,' she said.

'Sit down. I can see your baby came. You were not supposed to give birth here, that bed is so dirty!'

But Martha missed all that. She had not brought herself to this bed. She was brought here, and told to wait. How was she to know when her baby would come, and what she was supposed to have done?

They cut the flesh which joined them. They took the baby away. She wanted to follow them.

The baby was the only thing she had as her own. But she did not even have the strength to follow them to the bathroom. She was grateful when they brought it back. But also grateful because they had washed it. Its shining nose, and quiet kind eyes, and small mouth made her feel deep love for it. She put her nipple into its mouth. She laughed to see it suckle. It was as if it had been suckling for many, many years. She sat there on the wet bed with her baby suckling. They were waiting to go home, she and her baby.

Many other babies came that night, as she looked after little Mandela. They came as if this filthy place was a factory for mass-producing children. At dawn, Martha began to wonder: does this happen every day? Do babies come every day like this? When the sun came up, and the doctors came, and she was discharged, outside in the bright light she saw men coming to fetch the women with their bundles. She was happy to carry hers. She walked to where the kombis were. She was aching. But she reached the place and got to her mother. Her mother told her that there was no point in crying; she too had given birth to her, alone. Her father was in the mines in those days. They would look after the child. If God gave it to them, then they would be able to look after it. Yes, she was going to look after her baby.

But Lebo had said something else to her. No baby must be born in a filthy hospital, she thought. A white baby or a black baby must be born and looked after properly. Who would look after them? In that clinic near Soweto, there were no white babies. And there was no way that a baby could be born properly there. Yes, it would be good if all babies were born properly, but how? And Vino, how could she even begin to think about what Vino was saying. She was aware that her relationship with Vino was changing. It was no longer just student and teacher. They were becoming friends. For Vino it was easy. But for her, it was not easy. Vino had been her teacher; but besides, Vino is Indian. She has this long black hair; she looks properly looked after and knows so many things. No, this is not an easy thing to handle.

'Your baby is so lovely,' Vino had said. And Martha had agreed in one word. She had wanted to talk about this. But to think from

Xhosa to English takes a long time. To know what someone is saying in English also takes a long time. But also, outside of the single English words, which name things and point them out, how do you get to saying what you fear, feel, understand? So most times Martha was quiet; she said very little whenever Vino came to see her. Vino thought that Martha now and then laughed at wrong places in conversations. She did not understand. More so, because she knew that Martha was an intelligent woman. She wished she could speak in Xhosa.

She had seen how Martha's face and gestures changed when she conversed with other women in her class in Xhosa. 'You know, my bones, and many things in my body, are coming together,' Martha once said. Vino thought a while about this.

'How do you mean?' she asked.

'I'm healing,' she said.

Vino laughed, looking at Martha up and down. Martha laughed too.

'You have a man?' Martha asked.

'Yes, but I don't know what to do with him,' Vino said.

Martha thought for a while. 'Love him,' she said; 'you are lucky to have a man.'

'Lucky?'

'Yes.'

'What do you mean, "Lucky"? These men are mad,' Vino said.

'They are not mad, sometimes they are like children.' Martha wore an amused face.

'I know what you mean. You cook for them. You wash for them. You make up the bed for them, what are they supposed to do?'

'And then they trouble you all night,' Martha said, 'and leave you with Mandela.'

They both laughed. They leave you with Mandela, Vino thought, and laughed again.

'I would not mind if they left me with Mandela.'

'But how do you look after him if you are alone?'

'I see what you mean ...'

'You see?'
'Yes, I see.'
'It's heavy, don't you think?'
Vino laughed again.
'You know,' Martha said, her face lighting, 'when you give birth to a baby, it is like fire is lit all around here,' she said, gesturing to her loins, 'and the pain is like a sharp whistle, but large like the sky, and you think, this is the end of the world you know ...'
She could see that Vino was listening.
'You know, I was by myself, then, and the bed was wet and dirty. I wanted to go down the bed, up, under, I was afraid to scream, and I was alone, then, there was Mandela, crying and crying, loud, very loud, I laughed at him. I did not know what else to say. I picked him up, he was so filthy, but I kissed him, he is my child.'
'Where were the nurses?'
'I don't know. When one of them came, she shouted at me ...'
'Why did she shout at you?'
'She asked why I gave birth on the dirty bed.'
'But who put you there?'
'This man, I think he is a nurse or something ...'
'Why did he put you on that bed if it was dirty?'
'I don't know.'
Vino thought about this. The more she thought about it, the more she could not understand it. The more it angered her.
'So what happened then?'
'They cut this long meat which joined us, and took Mandela away to wash him. He came back looking at me with his big shining eyes ...'
'But they can't do that!'
'What?'
'They can't make you give birth on a dirty bed.'
'But they did.'
'Which hospital is this?'
'You know, the one near Soweto.'
'It's such a long time ago now, what a pity!'

'What do you mean?'

'It is not allowed what they did.'

'You mean the dirty bed?'

'Yes.'

'Well, if they thought we were people they wouldn't do it,' Martha said.

'We must fight things like that!'

'How?'

'If I knew about it when you gave birth, we should have gone to the hospital and raised the matter.'

'But I'm sure it did not start with me and it won't end with me,' she said.

'Actually, you are right,' Vino said.

There was silence.

They were looking at each other, and Martha, holding Mandela to the breast, kept closing one eye, so that she could focus, and look at him. Through their silence they tried to traverse their world.

'We always have been treated badly,' Martha said.

Vino thought about the manner in which Martha said 'We'.

'There is the fact that we all have to bring about a normal life; all of us,' Vino said, 'and, how and where do we begin?'

'No, I agree with you,' Martha said, 'and we have to know how to bring people together, but it needs us to know so many things.'

'Like what?'

'Like, you see, I am not educated; you are and I am poor and you are not,' she said.

'You are right about that, if in knowing that we want to know what it is that must bring us together.'

Martha put Mandela down and covered him with a soft blanket.

'Do you want more tea?'

'Yes,' Vino said.

'The struggle has brought many people together.'

She moved about the small room, rinsing the cups, boiling the water.

'That is very good,' she said, 'but what I am saying is that, for as long as there is a mind, there're blacks, there're whites, there're Indians, and there're those that are educated and those that are not educated, and those who are poor and those who are rich; there is still something which makes us different.'

'That is true, but should we not build on what makes us struggle together?'

'That too is true, but what I am saying is also true.'

They looked at each other. Mandela sighed, and Martha looked at him.

'To think that you are a mother now,' Vino said.

Martha smiled. 'What do you mean?'

'No, I mean that you have taken a major step.'

'You are younger than me, are you not? That's why you think so.'

'I am twenty-six,' Vino said.

'I am twenty-eight,' Martha said.

Both seemed to think about this for a while.

'I am now a widow,' Martha said.

'Pascal,' Vino said.

'Pascal introduced me to you.'

'Yes,' Vino said, 'he was such a hard worker. He brought me into the unions, and it is through him that I did adult education and started literacy campaigns for working women.'

'I used to feel so funny in those classes,' Martha said.

'Why?'

'They make you feel like a small child, you know.'

'Is that how you felt?'

'Ja.' She put the cups on the small table and poured the tea.

'But why is that?'

'I do not know, but they do,' Martha said.

'Is it what you learn about, or is it because of who is teaching you, or who you are learning with, what is it?'

'I don't know.'

'Would you still go back?'

'Ja, I learnt a lot, but it is difficult; the more you know something, the more you know how much you don't know,' Martha said.

'But education is like that,' Vino said; she was laughing.

'Maybe, but if you are old, and you are learning things which make you feel as if you are learning how to walk, it is not easy.'

'Yes, but Martha, what else is there to do?'

'No, I am just saying it is difficult.'

'I hear you,' Vino said. 'I am happy that we talked so much today.' She sipped her tea.

'Have you seen Lebo?' Martha asked.

'Ja. That one is so busy, I worry about her.'

'People in the struggle work very hard,' Martha said.

'But that is also because they are few.'

'I really never had lived with Pascal you know, he was so busy.'

'Now he is not here!' Vino said.

'How did you meet him?' Martha asked.

'He came once to our university, to talk to students; after the talk I went up to him. I told him what I wanted to study. He told me it was important. We kept in touch after.'

'Now that he is not here, I realize that he and I never really lived together,' Martha said thoughtfully, 'I sort of know him, but he lived in meetings and travelling.'

Vino and Martha had now come to realize the vast unexplored space between them. A space packed with unknowns. And silence fell upon them. Vino looked at her cup of tea as if she had never ever seen it before. Martha was thoughtful, looking at her fingers. The room was small, too small for anyone to shift, and the high bed on which Vino was seated turned into a trap; she could fall from it, and she was looking down upon Martha. Martha was not looking at her, she was looking at her thoughts, at her fingers and holding her cup away from her, in case the tea spilled, which also was a way of saying there was no space at all; the room was too small. She sat on a small bench.

It is a funny moment this. It is a moment when what you wish for, and what is real, conflict. It is a moment for brave people, who are also not afraid of the consequence of love; meaning, people who can also be honest. But then, warriors know, you can't always be honest. And, even if you still love, which is the consequence, you hold on to what cannot be said or done.

'The struggle has been very costly,' Vino said, breaking away from the moment.

'But of what use is the struggle if it neglected families?' Martha asked.

'For families to exist, there must be a normal society.'

'But normal society is made for normal families.'

'Ja.'

They looked at each other in silence. Vino wondered what right she had to pursue these issues.

'I don't know Pascal, and Mandela will never know him ...'

When they both lifted their eyes Lebo was standing at the door. She had a white plastic parcel. She was smiling. She tapped her feet on the mat, to remove dust from her shoes.

'Vino, you come to drink tea in servants' quarters?'

'I have come to see Martha and Mandela,' Vino said.

'Where's the old man?' Lebo said, as she uncovered Mandela who was sleeping peacefully.

'Lebo, don't wake him up.'

'Why?' She lifted the little boy up, kissed him on the cheeks, on the forehead, on the stomach and then held him back, far away from her, looking at him.

'Those cruel people, with their cultural weapons thought they were doing away with Pascal, here is Pascal,' she said, and kissed Mandela again.

'Martha, woman, how are you?' Lebo was smiling.

'I am fine,' Martha said.

'Your old lady tells me that she now and then finds you crying, why? A woman does not do that, you know. You don't know that a woman is a thing that holds a knife at its sharpest edge.'

'But sometimes it is so difficult!' Martha said.
'What is difficult?' Lebo asked.
'Haai, it's so difficult sometimes,' Vino felt left out of the conversation. Lebo was older than both of them. She had walked in and taken over.

'Hello ...' it was Carol, Martha's mother's employer. They looked at her, all of them, from their room. She could not walk in. There was no space.
'How's Mandela?' she asked.
'Fine,' Martha said.
'Lydia says he cries at night.'
'Not very much, if I give him milk he is okay,' Martha said.
'Lydia is Martha's mother?' Lebo asked in isiXhosa.
'Yes,' Martha said.
Something told Carol that she must go. She turned to go ...
'Martha, I will see you,' she said.
'Bye,' Martha said.
'That white woman must not call your mother by her first name,' Lebo said, 'she is a little girl.'
'Well ...' said Martha.

Rose Moss
A Gem Squash

Thin as a weed, Derek brings his own food in a cooler and re-packs it into Ruth's refrigerator, taking note of what she eats with disapproval. Ruth disapproves too. Food should be shared and bring people together, not say that her food is not good enough for him.

He puts a bottle of Poland Springs on the section of counter she uses for chopping.

No need to say anything now and give offense. She'll move it tomorrow if she needs the space. 'I notice you aren't changing filters as often as you should.'

'I've been told Cambridge water's clean.'

'You don't deny that it contains chlorine, and chlorine's carcinogenic.'

If it's not the Special Branch it's cancer.

She feels tempted to say, 'This obsession is so American.'

Nothing would insult him more. He has been damning Americans for thirty years, and does it now, impatient to expose the iniquity, 'Did you hear the radio? About the police torturing that Haitian prisoner?'

Of course she heard. It rang like a bell through her whole body, and is ringing still. As though she is back under apartheid and this is the only story, crying out to heaven with a voice of blood. Did you hear? You must hear.

Her parents told it. They talked about what was happening in the country, awed by the evil and the terror. 'Just like the Nazis.'

Of course Derek also hears the story ringing with stories like it.

The police torture. Kill a black child. Or – this is, after all, America – a Mexican child. For the same wanton desire to kick and injure, and be the beast on top that they both grew up with and cannot forget. 'Damn Americans.' America is the just object of his tireless fury.

One of these days she'll lose it and tell him it's time to grow up and see why the Wall fell. She holds her tongue. 'Wine?'

'Water. I've brought my own ... My nutritionist says I must drink a gallon a day.'

She hands him one of her blue Mexican glasses and a bowl of nuts, gestures to the soft white chair by the window and pours wine for herself.

'Are you going for tests this visit?'

'No. They say I'm all clear.' But not clear of trouble. 'I've got to see the tax people about going bankrupt.'

'So you've decided to do it.' Last spring he was investing in a pyramid scheme he hoped would bring in enough to pay off his debts. He's a babe in the woods. But what will bankruptcy mean? She sees nothing but darkness. 'Can you keep your cabin?'

'I think so ... I brought you some ashes. You must tell me where to put them tomorrow ...'

'Thanks for thinking of my garden.'

'Well, when you heat with wood ...'

'What time d'you see the tax people?'

'I've got to phone for an appointment.' Procrastinating? Maybe not. In need's tight grip he must count things like the cost of a long distance call. She's used to it.

He has picked up her *Times* and is leafing through it, looking for iniquities.

'Anything else? A pillow?'

He shakes his head, not needing her attentions. 'O.K. See you tomorrow. Take a shower if you like. You won't disturb me. Sleep late. It's your vacation you said.'

Throughout the night she hears his door swinging open and his steps to the bathroom. She sinks back into the dark water and pulls up again to the surface. A child is sick. No. Her sons are grown and gone now. She can sleep. He is coming back from the bathroom. He did not flush, fearing, perhaps, to wake her.

Does he have a flush toilet in Maine? How does he survive the dark months there, alone, sick.

She sinks under the surface again. A movement of water in the body flows into an ocean. Blood, darkness, furling over each other. Time flowing away, the medium of this short life.

He is going to the bathroom again. Like an old, incontinent man. Like her father in his last days. With no one by his side. Still a stranger in the country he came to. A man of suffering. Why are some people born to pain? To live forever without a home? Why is a Jew a Jew? A black, black? Can anyone change it?

She swims past shipwrecks. Schools of fish with dark faces open and close their mouths. No words, only shuffling, streaming. Something monstrous there beyond the crusted submarine, two men twisting another, head down to toes, yes baas.

Harsh crows announce dawn in her neighbour's maples, a jay gives its fierce call. They are not angry. Soon finches will come to her feeder for thistle seed.

She is drowsing now near Maseru, in a morning light. Hoepoes are courting on the yellow grass, and frost flows like threads of gold in the cream mountains. Heavy with the bag of rocks someone has hung on her back, she meets the eyes of other people. Also heavy laden. They know each other.

She moves the Poland Spring bottle to make coffee, then takes the steaming cup and paper to the patio where her red geraniums parade like toy soldiers. She begins to read. The Haitian prisoner is in critical condition, his intestines torn. The policemen were raping him with a toilet plunger. Like the Nazis, like the Nazis. Her parents' lament has fused with all these stories. She goes on. In Bosnia ... Underneath today's story, another that repeats her parents' lament as guards sort the men from the women and ...

She puts down the paper. Enough. Looks at the red geraniums. O.K. O.K.

When she picks up the paper again she chooses the stories. A huge real estate deal. A manoeuvre against the special prosecutor. Recipes using tomatoes. O.K. O.K.

She sets her mug in the dishwasher and walks toward her office. The bathroom door is closed and through the open door of the guest room she sees that Derek has spread pills and packages of nuts on the table, magazines on the floor.

Has he come without his shortwave radio? No sight of the heavy grey box he used to bring like a talisman, excusing himself every few hours to go off and listen to it alone, urgent for every detail, keeping notes. Last night, he did not listen to the news.

She stares out at her neighbour's red maples. As long as she's known Derek, he has listened to the news. Even after the *Fund for Justice* dissolved in a spate of quarrels and he stopped publishing the newsletter, he listened. Even after The Election, he clung to the news as though he must know, know now, know who. Something is happening to him. Perhaps he is trying to control his obsessions. Perhaps his nutritionist is telling him he can't have more than three newscasts a day.

Her heart rises in hope. Something should happen for Derek. Now that apartheid's over and there's nothing he can do for South Africa, something more gentle could happen.

She's even seen signs of it in his last few visits. The gift of woodash. Resignation about going bankrupt. Calling this visit to Boston a vacation. A shred of joy here and there.

She switches on the computer, opens her e-mail, answers a friend in London, and turns to the proposal she will take to the office tomorrow to show Jerry. It has to be on paper. He won't read off a screen. 'I can't see what it says,' he complains. 'It's what you're used to.' 'No, you actually can't see what it says until you see it on paper.' 'O.K. you're the boss.' Satisfied that they have this stuff between them, conversations, habits.

'*Môre, missies.*' Derek pokes his head in her office door, smiling.

'*Hoe gaan dit?*'

He's always enjoyed a few words of Afrikaans with her. The first time they met, in a small office the minister at Harvard set aside for anti-apartheid work, where students met to plan a Sharpeville commemoration and talk about the war, he said '*Voetsak,*' to her, smiling, the taste of home in his mouth. She was someone he did not have to explain to. They were so homesick.

They beam at each other. 'I'll have a cup of coffee with you,' she offers.

'My nutritionist says, no coffee. But join me.' Becoming her host.

She brews a fresh cup while he goes to the bathroom again. She sets a place for him in his colony of vitamins and remedies surrounding her salt and pepper. Chamomile. Garlic. Willow bark. With sovereign properties she used to read about in medieval texts when she was working on her dissertation. '*Pearl*, a fourteenth century mystical jewel.' He is still in the bathroom, and she goes back to her office to add a sentence to the proposal, listening for him.

She is not accustomed to coordinating with another person. It is a long time since the divorce, a long time since her last lover.

She begins a paragraph about the project's goals, and that calls for a change in the paragraph about its design, and ...

When she goes back to the kitchen, she finds him with the paper spread over the table, eating alternately from a large bowl of beige slurry and a black banana in his left hand.

'Americans don't know how to eat bananas. They should let them get black. That's when the starch breaks down into sugar and they get sweet.' He points to her bowl of fruit. 'You should never buy those yellow bananas. They're not ripe.'

Too much. To be preached at about bananas!

He sets his banana down and folds some of the newspaper away. She sits at the space he has cleared.

'United Fruit, those murdering swine. Capitalists. The CIA's still teaching torture ...'

By daylight, she sees that his skin is as pale as the oatmeal, or whatever it is, in her yellow bowl.

'How's your garden?'

He picks up the banana, takes a small bite, a spoonful from the bowl, and chews.

She talks, 'It's been tough here. A late spring, then drought. How about you? Enough for winter?'

'I couldn't plant much. With this chronic fatigue syndrome ... But my neighbours. These people in Maine. They are so kind. Last year, when I had my operation, Mike looked at my woodpile and said, You can't carry those big logs. He brought his sons over. A whole afternoon they spent splitting wood into small pieces I'd be able to carry. Can you imagine? And Anne brought over such a pie ... But with very little sugar.'

'They sound like good people.'

'Not like most damn Americans ... Mike said I must eat from their garden this year. They're putting stuff in a freezer in their basement. Gave me a key. There's generosity for you.'

'Is Mike the man who arranged for you to get some preaching?'

Her question dims his smile. 'He's got connections. He knows everybody in Maine.' Wistful. 'Good people.'

Another glimpse of sweetness. Perhaps through kind neighbours like these he will see what moves her in America, what she started to see when she gave up *Pearl* and recognized other people around her also doing what they must to earn money for their children.

While Derek has remained a lofty colonial, supercilious about the natives.

She wants to defend Americans working in factories and offices. Not ideological, they tend to their children and build their world bit by bit. They do not seem to need a story that makes sense of everything. They take explanations handy enough for making soap and packaging and improving market share. They wonder how to pollute less. All caught in the web of capitalism.

Derek sees nothing in capitalism but mine owners in houses with brilliant flower gardens and lawns green during a time of drought while at the hostels for migrant workers, men shovel mealiepap onto enamel plates, and push them at humiliated slaves. Capitalism is a miner who sleeps on a concrete bunk, in a cell with five others, owning little more than one set of clothes. Capitalism makes migrants everywhere, cuts husband from wife, mother from child.

Yes. That is true too. But now, capitalism seems a neutral force to her. She does not believe there is another more merciful. There is need, work, capital, greed – forces as powerful as gravity. Railing does not affect them. If anyone is ever to fly free, it will be by understanding what cannot be avoided, by something ingenious and not discovered yet, something you can't think of until you can almost do it, like how to make steel fly lighter than air.

'I'm working today, but if there's something you want ... You can use this phone to call the tax people.'

'Have you got a telephone book?'

'In my office.'

He follows her, she hands him the directory, and he lingers, looking at other books. Not only about the moral universe of suffering and evil, love and courage where apartheid is the key pattern of evil, repeating in her own life what happened to her grandparents and happens still. To the Haitian prisoner.

She will never lay down this weight, but now the books in her office are about computers and genetics. When she learned technical writing, she started to see the world a new way, not only as the moral universe of suffering and courage. Now she saw an alphabet of utmost simplicity that can express utmost subtlety, and as another code, an alphabet for writing the words that make life.

The great work of her time is a human endeavour to master these alphabets. She began to be glad she was in America, near the heart of this work.

When she read about what was driving technology she glimpsed yet another power to master. Communism and Capitalism changed under her eyes from a choice of the poor against the rich, the suffering against the powerful, into a choice of techniques. Both try to map and navigate oceans of desire and need. The code of that turbulence is still hidden, not like the digital code and the genetic code. She began to think, if I had another lifetime, that's what I'd like to learn.

For this lifetime, she believes now, the moral choice remains, but wise choice must acknowledge the nature of things.

'Can I borrow this?' He holds out a memoir by someone who grew up in Kroonstad.

'Take it. I don't know when I'm ever going to read it.' She feels ashamed of the casual gesture that makes her rich, him poor.

Derek's choice has also been the great work of their time. Justice is the great work of every time.

In the hours that follow she hears him going to the bathroom again, probably reading there, unaware of anyone else.

In the middle of the morning, she wanders back to the kitchen for a last cup of coffee.

'Do you want this article?' About sweatshops. He has underlined long passages. 'I want to cut it out.'

'Go ahead,' tasting again the rancid ease of a gift without cost.

She returns to the proposal wondering what he does all day in Maine.

The end of apartheid has stranded him here in America, where an encompassing ideology seems strange to the temper of people, and he has little work. Two sermons a week. Two hundred dollars. For thirty years he gave every day to the cause, and now it is gone.

At The Election, he went back. 'I've got a passport for the first time in my life,' but when he came back, he did not talk of returning to live in South Africa. The main story he told her was about a man he sat next to on the plane from Cape Town to Durban.

'Aren't you Derek Wardell?'

'How do you know ?'

'I know you, man. I got your picture in your dossier. I'm with the Special Branch since 1965. I know you better than you know your own hand, man. No hard feelings, hey.'

'You still with the SB?'

'No man, I'm retired. Just in time. Jirre! I never thought I'd meet you like this. Everything's upside down now.'

It must have been a strange visit, fulfilling a lifetime of longing and showing him, however that happened, that he could not go back to the country he still calls home.

'What a meeting, Derek! What did you do when he told you?'

'We had a beer together and talked about how the times are upside-down. You know what he kept saying? 'It's like the Bible says.'

'What did he mean?'

'He wanted me to tell him, as a minister, if it was the end of the world.'

'It was the end of his world, for sure. "I will cast the mighty aside in the conceit of their hearts and will fill the poor with good things." Isn't that how it goes? You think he meant that? That the prisoner would be president?'

'Those guys knew what was going on. They knew.'

'What was it like to talk to him?'

'Like meeting the Angel of Death and thinking he's just a human being like me. He *was* my Angel of Death. He had my whole life in his records.'

'I suppose there's something he didn't know. As you say, he's just a human being.'

For Derek too, everything in the way he saw his future must have turned upside-down.

More and more she believes that if God exists at all, it is as One Who Is invisible, present, everywhere hidden.

He has been leafing through the magazines by the white chair, making heaps of pieces he wants to tear out.

She rolls her head from side to side, 'I need a break. Let's go down to the farmstand and get fresh corn. It's almost a sin not to eat it in August. They'll have butter-and-sugar.'

'American corn is so sweet.' She can't tell, is that good or damned?

'As a kid, I used to long for mealie season,' she confides. 'Mealies, and the first rain.'

'God, yes, the first rain.'

Her mother believed the children must wait for the first rain before it was safe to go swimming. After that first blissful downpour streaming from hair to face they could go to the municipal swimming pool. Then, endless under the sky, blue and receding and near and blue, blue, the water, the sky, distant, pure, forever, as she floated and stared, the sun dazzling, the water tender, silent and happy, time without history, without smirch, without fear, simply being, being alive.

She has never seen such blue outside South Africa.

Derek, the fanatic for what should be, exclaims 'Children long with such passion. Can you imagine what the world would be like if we longed like that for justice?'

After longing for swimming, the children longed for mealies. The taste of butter and kernels connected them to Sunday afternoon drives to the Hartebeestpoort Dam and Parys and huge skies building cumulus clouds with heavy bellies flattened on the lower layer of air.

In dry Johannesburg, their mother sighed for misty fields by a river, for mushrooms in the woods, northern berries, cucumbers, the white nights of summer and fresh snow where she would beat herself with birch branches after bathing in steam.

At weddings, there'd be a table where *landsleit* gathered for gossip and nostalgia. The children went off to find others impatient with their parents' conversation.

He is willing to risk one ear of corn. She pulls the husks, leaving one layer over the plump seeds for flavor.

'Remember loquats?'
'We're like my parents with their *landsleit*.'
'What's *landsleit*?'

When she was growing up, at the dinner table in Yeoville, stories thickened around words like Hitler and pogrom. At Purim her mother baked poppyseed *hammantaschen*, and said that Haman wanted to exterminate the Jews like the Nazis. When Ambrose, the gardener, asked for a note with permission to come home after eleven, her father told her Jews used to need permission to travel. Cossacks would tear up Jews' papers for spite and spit on parents in front of their children.

With Derek here today, she is living in the pattern of her parents, half in Vilna, half in Johannesburg; half in South Africa, half in New England. She and Derek are creatures of the same species, amphibians under water with their nostrils in the air. It is not so strange after all that they have become friends who last with each other when so much else falls away.

They understand each other.

Living in the North, she sees why people from the South feel misunderstood. She finds her friends among Americans who live now out of the places they were born to, gay men from Texas and the midwest, journalists who have had their minds turned on Indian reservations. Her other friends are foreigners, Czechs who could not go home after '68, Chinese born in Hong Kong, an Indian from Bombay. She finds herself among people who have been colonized, who have travelled labyrinths, who know daily that they must live in a world where they will be misunderstood.

She has found it more difficult to make friends among blacks here than it was under apartheid. Segregation seems to happen here without agents, without the guns and laws of South Africa, without the laws and trains of the Nazis. Something more secret and diffuse in America makes its apartheid stronger.

Perhaps America really does reproduce apartheid, as Derek says, and she is blind here, like so many people she knew in South Africa. Blind, and would not see. Perhaps she is too comfortable now, too happy. She has heard about the Haitian prisoner and read about him, but her day is full of pleasure. If she can live with such suffering and be calm after all, isn't she damned, just as he says?

How can anyone live in this world where there is so much suffering and where you can still go out on a sunny day to buy butter-and-sugar corn and take it home to eat with a friend?

She has disappointed Derek. When they were out buying corn, he wanted a detour to buy a German beer he cannot find in Maine. Like the ascetic missionaries she knew near Maseru, he allows himself one daily indulgence, a beer, and gives the choosing and enjoying of it – of course it is not American and he drinks it warm – the attention of a gourmet. He knows just the pilsener that yields the finest pleasure, and she feels this sensuality important and human. He is not a cold disapprover of other people's pleasures, not part of the bitter Christianity they used to see every Sabbath when the city fell silent before a frowning God. 'There's a liquor store just round the corner.'

They find his favourite pilsener, but he wants to repeat a hour of companionable shopping in a large discount store they visited last spring.

'Not today, Derek. I've got to get back to work.'

'Isn't it on the way?'

'It is five miles away. Twenty minutes at least.' Closing a gate that keeps him outside her work and place in this world.

He has never worked for money.

They cannot share the day's abundance. She feels it shrink into a garden with brilliant flowers that a high wall hides from the open world.

'Did you see the editorial about the sweatshops?'

'I did.'

'Damn Americans.'

'Derek, there's something funny about the way you see things. Millions of people wish they could be Americans. They wish they could live here. They risk their lives to come.'

'Don't you remember how they used the same argument against us in South Africa?'

'But here it's not like Africa, from greater misery.' Made by capitalists and colonial powers. She knows his script. 'People come from Europe and Asia, with talent and education. So many want to come to America. How can you think you know better than everyone else?' Deepening the personal edge to her disagreement.

'Because I do know better.'

'Oh then, well, of course, I have to agree.'

He leaves the room, and his straight back catches her eye. An English gentleman does not bow to injury but bears up.

Dammit, why couldn't I hold my tongue? How could I talk to him like that? Such an old friend. Going through such a hard time?

When he comes back to the room, proud and smiling, he says, 'It's good we could make a joke.'

'Ag, man.' But she's drawn blood, she fears. What a mess. No one else shares all these years. They were together when Verwoerd was assassinated, when the Portuguese gave up, when Biko was killed. During the treason trials they called each other. He was the prophet who told her, 'De Klerk is a man of faith and knows what he is called to do.'

She is still repenting when he says, 'I'm off to the Divinity School to buy some books and meet Clive.'

'Old haunts and old friends, hey? See you later, then.' Wanting to sound warm, not crotchety like before.

He bears his straight body with ease now and could stroll out to a game of cricket wearing that cotton shirt and quiet decorum of men who know themselves masters.

No wonder America remains shocking to him. People must take as privileged what he takes as normal. Few can see the privation that is making him sweet, working in him like a yeast, making him more tolerant and forgiving.

Sometimes, she thinks, God, if there is a God, will do anything to get a person straight, even if it means breaking every limb in his body.

Whatever God is up to, if there is a God, it remains inscrutable and she sets to finishing the proposal. The work engrosses her like a pleasure and she stops only when the screen blurs. She stands and looks out at the red maple trees on her neighbour's lawn, the flux of thought still moving muscles under her mind, until objects regain clear outlines.

When Derek comes in, she is still working, 'I'll just be a minute,' and hurries to finish.

After the save command, she finds him reading the weekend magazine. 'Are you finished with this?'

'Why?'

'I want to cut out an article.' She guesses it is the piece on deaf Mexicans lured to New York and enslaved to sell trinkets on subway stations. Another iniquity.

'Have it,' with a pang that he asks her permission. After his life of sacrifice and work, this stinting poverty. South Africa and her parents' stories have taught her never to believe that wealth equals merit, as so many Americans do. 'You deserve...' they say. Not believing that everything is an accident or a gift. Not imagining that they could be too wretched to earn or deserve. Not knowing, as Derek does, that this world does not judge as God judges. If God exists, she believes, the One Who Is is working quietly through a code more simple and abundant than anything Americans know. Or anyone knows. The one probable sign to the mind is paradoxes. And to the heart, love.

'Clive gave me a wonderful thing.' He has put it on the kitchen counter for her to admire. 'A gem squash.' A dark green globe like a small, mysterious grapefruit.

Her mother also loved gem squash, and did not hanker to be in another place when she had it on her plate.

'Where on earth did he find a gem squash in America?'

'In his own garden. He smuggled in seeds.'

'What a treasure for you. He's lucky they don't train dogs to sniff the seeds in airports.'

'It's not cocaine.'

'If it was, you'd be able to buy it here.'

'He gave me two. I'm saving one, but we should share one.'

She resists the urge to refuse, to say that gem squash means nothing to her and so much to him he should enjoy it all himself. It is important to share, to give companionship as she takes the holy food. Especially today, when she has cut him and he is forgiving her. Choosing reconciliation, like a South African.

She contemplates the orb that holds the world he longs for. It is a small sphere without lustre.

'How should we cook it?'

As they eat it, steamed, with butter and salt and pepper, the way her mother loved it, Derek tells her about his first year in the ministry.

'I was much younger than most ministers, you know. There was a good priest in Kingwilliamstown, and he told me to go to university first, but I was so determined ...Then there was a crisis, and they needed someone in the circuit near Thaba 'Nchu, so they asked if I'd go. They gave me a collar and permission to distribute the eucharist. It wasn't really allowed for someone who wasn't ordained yet, but they did it.

'That was the first time I went into a township. There were two churches of course. A big stone one, almost empty. Six people came to the eucharist. And another church in the township. So I went there. What a shock!'

He must have seen something like the crowded shacks of corrugated iron she used to see. Smoke. A chicken scavenging. Children with their fists in their mouths. Skeletons with swollen bellies.

Still in primary school, she watched two picannins searching rubbish bins in the street outside, taking out half eaten mealie cobs. Outside the Coliseum with its starry sky and artificial scraps of cloud, she saw picannins dancing for money. One played a penny whistle. They wore men's jackets gaping over bodies as bony as prisoners' in the newsreels of concentration camps she had just seen.

She never got used to it, and then there was more. More. Always more suffering. At a settlement of tents on the banks of a dried out river, a child playing in a puddle next to the dirt road, the smell of urine, someone saying, 'They have to drink that, you know.' The next day at the mission hospital, her first corpse, a child dead of gastroenteritis.

Derek continues, indignant as though he is still in that circuit, just in from that township, 'And the church itself! Just a room of corrugated iron. The roof was rusting away. The rain was coming through. The floor was mud. People kneeled on that floor to pray. Their faith, their faith ...' His voice full of awe. Tender as a man in love.

That's what keeps him going. All the lonely years, this gold has been shining in him like a river of God. That's why he hates America. So much outward piety, so little of what he has seen as faith, hope, compassion.

'That wasn't all. After the service, a Coloured parishioner came to me. He said, "I know how little money they give you young ministers. I've been giving five pounds a month to the one who was here before you, and I want you to take five pounds from me now." So there I was, a white man, taking charity from a Coloured. That was a shock too.'

He relishes it, sweet as the gem squash luscious with butter. Nourishing him with something better than justice.

'The third thing ... It's not everyone who has the chance to know when they open a dossier on you, but that's what happened to me. I preached about the township, and one of my six white parishioners came to me, worried. He was my age, working for the police and expecting to join the Special Branch. It was his circuit too. He wanted to warn me. If I went on preaching like that, I'd get into trouble.

'I had the whole country there. Everything clear in that one circuit.'

That country she knows as hers. Where she saw people at prayer and felt awed at their dignity. In a church in Ladysmith where her nanny had gone to die, women wearing blankets kneeled on bare mud, concentrating and still. Children of God. Their posture alone affirmed trust. Not railing about justice, they set aside the judgement of this world where victory goes to the bullies. They held such peace in their bodies that, looking at them, she saw why artists invented haloes to suggest that quality, luminous and shining like gold. They could not know why they must live as the wretched of the earth, as

131

Jews do not know why they are chosen, afflicted and persecuted. Not for what they have done, the Nazi notion, and not because they deserved it, the simple American idea. By an inscrutable choice or by accident. If there is no God, working in the world in a subtle code, if it is all an accident and does not mean anything, there is no justice and no hope. But, even with no God, nothing can take from her mind's eye the dignity of those women praying. Her faith in their faith. Derek's story brings back that morning when the veld was white with frost on the brittle grass and wind knifed through the church. Her hands burned with cold, her feet were heavy with pain. She did not know how long she would be able to sit on the chair one of the women had brought for her because she was white and must not kneel on the mud.

She and Derek came from the same place. He must have had an African nanny like hers. They grew from the same womb, were formed in the same code, like brother and sister.

In all these years far from her first home, he has been there, but she did not know why.

'Thanks for sharing the gem squash with me. It was great.' The American word irks her like a lie, uneasy in the company of her gratitude that Derek has shown her where she is rooted, what she believes.

She wishes she had led his life. Dedicated to serving these poor.

With this ending?

She has been like an American looking at his life and seeing that he is poor. But the God of the poor who calls him is, after all, the one who fed Elijah, renewing the meal at the bottom of the widow's barrel one handful at a time, and the oil drop by drop, until the end of the drought. Derek has enough.

Does his preaching reach to the heart like this in Maine? Another country where people live one handful at a time, and understand that money does not reveal merit.

'Tell me about your congregations.'

'I'm afraid I may lose one of them.'

'How come?'

'I went to see the Berrigans, and talked with them about their protest at the nuclear submarine. I preached about the millions, billions of dollars spent on military projects like that without need, when there are so many people who do need. It offended people in the congregation. Not the comfortable, but the working class. I had to preach. It was just like my sermon about the township.'

She cannot hold her tongue. She wants to protect him. She wants to scold him. She wants to save him from the faith at the core of his life, the faith she has just felt she shares.

'Oh Derek, why do you have to be a prophet? You're a Jeremiah. They'll stone you.' She wants to stone him herself.

Lionel Abrahams
Enemy

A strange elation overtook Felix a few minutes after he had bumped into Willem Prinsloo one day in town. Over the years, chance meetings with other former fellow-inmates of the Home had usually rather depressed him, reminding him too keenly of how disliked he had felt there ("unpopular" was the word used then), how often displaced and endangered. Yet Willem Prinsloo was the bully he had particularly hated and feared, while most of the other boys in the senior section for children over fourteen had shared his feelings, had been his allies against the tyrant.

His throat contracted when he recognized the robust man limping toward him across Harrison Street with a young woman on his arm. He had often toyed with fantasies of facing him in the grown-up world, but now that it was really about to happen he did not know what to expect. He was trembling a little as he spoke the first words of greeting.

'Willem ... Hullo. How goes it?'

'No, it's okay with me, thanks. And you?'

The perfectly civil answer amounted to a reprieve, and not now needing to escape, Felix dared, 'And what are you doing nowadays?'

'Oh, diamond cutting, you know ...' There was no sarcasm, though Felix ought to have remembered, that being the trade many of the boys became apprenticed to. Willem added, 'This is my wife.'

And so, with a minute of cool politeness while they waited for a robot's permission to move on, the encounter passed and they walked away from each other. Perhaps it was simply relief that accounted for the elation that now swept Felix up. There had been, on Willem's part, none of the old harshness or rudeness or menace, and no sign of recrimination – and this softening might have had to do with his wife's presence, the public place, or some ten years of forgetting. But on his own part, Felix was surprised to discover a complete freedom from bitterness. So there was more to his little euphoria than just relief. That decade-old toxic element in his memories of Willem seemed suddenly to have been neutralized. He allowed himself a fanciful regret that he had not invited the pair to join him for a snack in a nearby cafe, so that once more, after so long, he and Willem might eat at the same table. How different it would have seemed, how delicious the contrast with those many meals at the long tables when all he wished from Willem was not to be noticed by him.

Why had he been so daunted? It must have been some particular degree of unripeness in his adolescent outlook that had induced him to hug his fear and caricatured Willem into a monster. Reflecting now on the face he had just re-encountered, Felix found no quality there, after all, that necessarily bespoke brutality and arrogance. Those quick-moving eyes under the brow that so readily rumpled in heavy frowns, need not seem fierce or suspicious. He recalled noticing just such features on someone he knew only as mild and tractable.

And Willem's gestures and habits also appeared in a new light. Even the way, with his grin or laugh, his tongue-tip would protrude, pressed against his lower lip as though to restrain his eagerness, keeping the curve wet and hungry-looking, had lost its malign aspect. Felix had recognized that old habit, when it had reappeared while they chatted, with something like a secret greeting for itself.

But he could remember how in the old days when Willem Prinsloo laughed, when his tongue-tip showed and his bull voice leapt up the scale into a shrieking giggle, smaller boys would melt with terror. It made Felix smile. What queer exaggerations had stifled their reason and moused their courage. How grossly their lack of perspective had distorted reality.

In the hierarchy of physical strength that framed the society of thirty or forty boys at the Home Willem Prinsloo's place was at the summit. Felix's was usually near the bottom. The only boys on whom he could impose his will were bed-patients – like Nemus Marais, who was paralysed from his chest down and who died during his second winter there. He was a thoughtful, older boy with gentle manners whom Felix like to chat with and play at chess, draughts or Chinese checkers. Yet from time to time, he could not resist teasing Nemus a little, pretending to try to push a cake of soap into his mouth, amused by his helpless giggles and breathless protests as they came by turns.

But Willem Prinsloo, with his cabinet of strong henchmen, ruled the whole community. And regarding him from his station in the system Felix was bound to perceive him wrongly. He figured as a simple, all-powerful instrument of motiveless cruelty, at once despicable and fearful. Felix would freeze in a stupor of dismay as Willem appeared and strode toward him, bawling one of the contemptuous nicknames he favoured – 'Joodjie ... Pigmeat ... Proffessorr ...!'

What followed was often a treacherous game. Taking his subject gently into the strong circle of his thick arm, Willem would adopt an almost fatherly tone, murmuring, 'Come on, come on, Joodjie, it's about time I got you a bit tough. Let's teach you how to take it, eh ...' Then he would begin, flicking Felix's ears with his finger-nails, perhaps, grappling knee muscles with timber-hard hands, punching biceps, blowing illicit cigarette smoke into his face ... There was always the chance that his mood would push him across a certain boundary, and he would bring the burning end of his cigarette closer and closer to blistering point, until enough terror showed, or he would rub with a moistened thumb at a spot on Felix's hand until the skin broke and was left to leak and fester ...

'I'm only playing with him,' he invariably explained if any of the staff happened on the scene ...

With his new perspective, Felix judged that he would feel quite differently about such things if he had to undergo them again, far less negatively. After all, the bully only rarely inflicted a real injury. The way things appeared now, if Willem puffed smoke at him, the knowledge that cigarettes were strictly forbidden to the boys would add, to his sense of grazing up against Life as he choked and struggled to turn his face away, a touch of admiration, a tickle of mirth at Willem's bravado. And he played with the thought that the other ex-inmates of the Home, similarly broadened by experiences of life away from that protected hilltop, ought also to see the remembered Willem cloaked in this benign numbus of revised appreciation. When, with the benefit of maturity and detachment, they recalled the things he had done to them, they ought to chuckle nostalgically, or even feel grateful.

There was, for instance, the tall, big-boned fellow whom Willem once dealt a black eye. Granted some perspective, that boy might find the memory more than a little amusing – especially recalling that the bruises round his eye were outlasted by the days that Willem's sprained fist had had to be wrapped in sticking plaster – and laugh out loud while rocking on his callipered legs and crutches.

And the feelings of the dwarfish boy whom Willem had swung round in the air while holding him by the ankles should be, whenever he looked back on the incident, a surge of gratitude for a unique experience. Counting up the number of times his head touched the floor as he whirled round and round through that switchback circle, his gratitude should grow in proportion to Willem's ingenuity and determination and strength.

And so, through the ranks of all who had lived in fear of the top dog's whims. All would be able to recall his "punishments" and "lessons" in a light, positive spirit, instead of with the bitterness of victims. Ripeness had surely endowed them with the same genial balance that Felix now felt he enjoyed.

In those days, however, his outlook had been as distorted and narrow as any. It was as though, somehow, he had remained fixed for months and years in the after-effects of his first fright from Willem: as still a new boy, he'd been jerked awake one night by the suffocating pressure of a heavy hand clapped over his nose and mouth, while the dark simmered with giggling. While he kicked and squirmed, Willem muttered in his ear, as though giving some kindly advice, 'Suffocation ... You shouldn't of told anybody this is what you scared of.'

He had led a gang of pyjamaed raiders from upstairs to give the smaller boys' dormitory a little skrik, just for fun, just to remind everyone who was boss. But the shock had left Felix unnerved and bitter. In the shallow soil of his inexperience he had, after that, rooted an unrealistic tree of heroic righteousness. He conscientiously hated Willem with the abhorrence of a Round Table Knight for villainy. He cherished dreams of revenge; and meanwhile, whenever it seemed possible to do so, he regarded it as an honour to foil the bully.

That was why, when he had seen him swinging that pigeon-chested boy by his ankles and heard the thump that came each time his skull bounced on the floor, he had burst noisily into tears and created so much surprise – perhaps it had never before happened that one boy cried because of something that was being done to another – that Willem had stopped what he was doing and turned to growl, 'What the blerry hell's the matter with you ...? Shut your bek or I'll donner you,' before stomping out of the common-room.

And then there was Basil, the Catholic boy with the good singing voice who slept in the next bed to Felix's in the downstairs dormitory. When Willem had wanted to push Basil in his wheel-chair around the building to the quiet, hidden part of the lawn, and then to undo the hank of rope he always had hanging from his Scout belt and fold it into a thick lash, and then to have one of his henchmen take Basil out of the wheelchair and place him on all fours on the grass, and then to – when Willem announced that intention to his justice committee, Felix found that he had to intervene. He came out with, 'No, Willem, don't give him lashes. Basil's weak and you might damage him seriously.'

'What the hell you talking about? You shut up. He's got to be punished.'

'Yes, sure. But, Willem, listen, I know what ... Just let us tell him that on Wednesday after supper you are going to take him and there and do that ...'

'What you mean?' Willem demanded. 'He's got to have his punishment. There's got to be no stealing from lockers.'

'Yes, I know. But he will be punished.' And then Felix explained how they would let Basil wait three days in suspense, and how at the end of that time, on Wednesday after supper, they would have him wheeled out to that hidden part of the lawn as though that were the time for it, and how only then Willem would tell him that he had been punished enough.

'That won't teach him not to steal.'

'Oh yes, it will,' Felix pointed out. 'It will be even worse than the other.'

Willem looked at him suspiciously. 'But listen here,' he growled, 'I'll break your blerry neck if you tell him we not really going to punish him. Hoor jy!' Then he told someone to go and fetch Basil into his presence.

The reason for Felix's sudden promotion to Willem's counsels was that it was his locker that had been robbed. It was his purse with his one-and-tenpence in it that had disappeared. He had hunted for it and told the boys of his dormitory. The word had got to Willem, their policeman, judge and executioner, and he had summoned all the boys into the common-room and commanded them to own up, and in the usual way had been met with a sheepish silence. Then he had ordered a search of all downstairs lockers. It was fruitless, but afterwards the purse had been found under Basil's mattress.

The recovery of the purse satisfied Felix, but of course it meant the finding of a culprit, and that demanded Willem's judicial attention. 'There's got to be no stealing from lockers,' he proclaimed. 'Anyone who steals from lockers has got to be severely punished.'

Basil, the dormitory's songbird, omitted his usual ritual of singing softly to his room-mates after lights-out that night. In fact, he remained very quiet during the whole of those three days leading to Wednesday evening. He sat drooping in his wheelchair, bothering to drive himself only when and where he was compelled to. His eyes avoided every face, and his answers to anyone who addressed him were short and absent.

When Felix saw that no one else was nearby he came close and said, 'Listen, Basil don't be anxious about what is going to happen on Wednesday. Believe me, you don't have to worry about it. I ...' Basil gave a start, thrust out his trembling lower lip, glared for a moment, then turned his head aside without answering a word, and began to propel himself away. It was the same the other two or three times Felix tried to pass him a hint about the real state of affairs. 'Look, about old Willem and Wednesday after supper, you don't have to ...' But each time a surge of blind fear and anger made it impossible for Basil to take in the comforting news.

On Wednesday at sunset, when he was wheeled round the building to the hidden part of the lawn his face was very pale. And it became even paler when Willem lifted him out of his wheelchair and put him on all fours on the grass, then ordered a hanger-on to hold Basil steady while he got ready. Then he undid the hank of rope on his belt, folded it to the right length for the lash, and tested it noisily two or three times on his hand. But Basil's features retained that greenish shade even after he had been lifted back into his wheelchair and Willem had announced to him that he had been punished enough, and explained, 'But, hoor jy, Basiltjie, next time you won't get off like this if I ever hear you been stealing again. I know you always praying, but that's not gonna help you. There's got to be no stealing from lockers.'

While he was giving each of the little justice committee a smile of gratitude and relief Basil's cheeks remained pale, and immediately he was done he hung his head. As soon as he could suppose that no one was watching him, Felix saw him cross himself and mutter something with shaking lips. That night again, there were no songs in the dormitory after lights out. Basil had climed into bed and gone to sleep very early.

Looking back on it all from the vantage of his new perspective on Willem Prinsloo, Felix saw how a similarly broader vision might have opened Basil to happier possibilities. Instead of being so shocked and angry, so damaged because he had let himself be terrified, Basil might at least have relished the relief of his reprieve. And he might have taken a little comfort from the realization that after all, Willem was not absolutely and uncontrollably dangerous. He might even have appreciated a kind of joke in the charade he had been through. The lesson Willem had intended might have been the least of what he had learnt about life that evening in the hidden corner of the lawn. And he would have given that half-hour after lights out to singing, to more exuberant singing than usual. And might, out of something between mockery and gratitude, have sent someone upstairs with a note to Willem, inviting him to come down in his pyjamas and listen to the recital.

At that time, nothing would have been stranger to Felix than the idea of Basil reacting in any such way. The victim's restricted vision was equally his own. Indeed, his perspective on Willem was even narrower and gloomier than Basil's and everyone else's. He was on their side and against Willem. He even felt, as perhaps the favourite subject of his attentions, that he was secretly their leader against the tyrant. In some way, it was left to him to exact retribution for all his crimes. He dreamed of a distant day when they would be men and Willem would somehow be in his power, and he would darkly and mercilessly torture him until he had exacted frrom him as much agony as he had squeezed from their hearts.

That was why, on that Sunday some weeks after Willem had left the Home to take up his diamond cutting apprenticeship, when according to the custom of old boys he paid the place a visit, his reception was so unceremonious that this first visit was also his last. When Felix glanced around himself that Sunday afternoon, he found that all the boys on the lawn were gathering and forming themselves into a crescent behind him, like a Zulu impi.

'You, Willem Prinsloo,' he shouted, 'listen, I'm going to tell you a few things ... And you're an outsider now, don't think you can bully any of us any more ...'

As his taunts and insults poured forth, his limbs trembled uncontrollably, but his voice remained so strong that he felt it could flood the whole huge plane beneath them with Willem's humiliation. And though he saw that face darken and twist in anger, those huge legendary fists fold up into terrible hammers, he knew that now the bully was impotent against them, so nothing could stop his tirade, which went on until Willem turned and began to limp away, shouting over his shoulder, 'You going to hear from me. I'll see you with the police! Just wait ...'

Since that day Felix had not seen him again and lately rarely thought of him until this casual crossing of paths with Willem as an ordinary pedestrian walking arm in arm with his wife. So he was surprised at how a bare minute of contact in Harrison Street, alongside the City Hall, could change his feelings from that last rancorous triumph to this broadminded and worldly forgiveness. No, to an emotion even more positive than that. For the truth was that Felix found himself suffused – as he threaded his way among streams of strangers who were excluded from the experiences Willem Prinsloo and he had lived through together – with a feeling of brotherliness towards him.

Es'kia Mphahlele
Silences

August 1992-1993

Silence is explosion
of sperm and egg in the womb creating life;
is mother suckling baby
with its hand resting featherweight
on her breast in divine two-way contentment;
is the pulse of the stars and other
spheres in their endless orbits;
is the Nile, the Niger, Zaire, Zambesi, Limpopo,
even as they flow unhurried down the plains
or cascade over boulder, precipice
in a perpendicular plunge.
Somewhere the Silence will return
when waterways survive the thunderous fall
and flow with self-abandon
into the sea's embrace, their journey's end.

Silence is the Infinite with many names,
the One Unknowable Vital Force
that dwells in each of us.
Listen my brothers and sisters
to the silence ...

Silence is a chain of moments
when a soldier takes Death
by the throat on the battlefield,
but loses out and yet Eternal Silence
wraps him up,
woven for him by compassionate Death
waiting always at the bend of the road.

Silence is the patient's body
immersed in a liquid of pain
that holds her hostage on her bed;
is the slow movement of glazed eyes
that tell you
the cruel thing you do not want to hear:
'You my husband, you my children, you my friend,
all of you around my bed,
I do not know you any more:
this leaping fiery pain has made strangers of us,
me to you, you to me ... you can never carry it for me ...
I cannot feel your fear for me, but let it be ... let it be ...'

Silence is the body's final surrender
and its unrelenting descent
into the mouth of the earth
that holds the afterbirth
of newly-born arrivals.

Silence is the sap that floods the plant,
the rain that pushes it upward
to suck the open sun and air
down its inner chemistry:
the silent miracle of growth.

Silence was the agony and sorrow
of the Man of Nazareth
hanging on a tree and bleeding to save mankind

from what believers never truly comprehend
who tell us the news, never will,
till the end of time.
For millions have created God
and the man on the cross in their own image,
millions of tongues
have told the story of salvation
in as many ways in endless sermons
that have deadened many hearts –
a song trapped in the groove of a broken disc.

Silence is the desert dunes
panting under the broiling Arabian sun
where the trader-poet-Prophet
recited divine revelations to Mecca and Medina
and far abroad.
As with the followers of the Man from Nazareth,
those of the desert Prophet also twisted
their teacher's message
for greed and for power.
One jihad after another
of sword and spear and arrow,
and later death riding on missiles
and desert tanks – all made mockery
of the Holy Silence.

Silence is the Universal Self
to which we surrender
our single little selves
to feel the healing touch of the Infinite.
'For our universe,' says the Oriental sage,
'is the sum total of what
the person knows, imagines, reasons to be.'
All of us must strive towards
that Magnificent Silence

of the ages that sings
the mysteries of Nature and our own existence.

Silence is divine delight
when we find ourselves in others
in an act of love.
It is not that I love my son or my daughter,
says the Hindu sage,
but that I seek my soul in them.

Silence is the wanderings
and reflections of Gautama of Nepal –
centuries before the Man from Nazareth –
in the valley of the Ganges,
learning from teachers
the many ways that lead to
the greatest good;
is Gautama's departure from his teachers
to seek his own silence under
the Tree of Wisdom,
which made him the Buddha,
the Enlightened One;
silence is his mission
to find The Way.

Silence is the all-enfolding
universal spirit
Hindu calls Brahma,
the infinite that is also the ever-revolving
cycles of unity and harmony
in the world of humans.
To be in harmony with the Mahatma the Great Soul,
says the Hindu sage,
the single little soul will find

its greatness in unity
with all the others.

Silence is dominion of our ancestors
watching over Africa:
the heroes now gone beyond
to the land of absolute peace;
is our family members also in
the Great Beyond,
who take our words of gratitude
and supplication
to One Supreme and Infinite.

Silence is the highest possible
good in us —
Super Soul that others give the name of God;
is the cycles of our inner will
to be in touch with our being;
is the crossing of the midnight zone
to hear the crowing of the cock
when the sleeper's breathing measures
the steady pulse of tranquillity.

Silence attends
each birth
and is surprised by
the bawling of the newly born,
is the revolving drama of joy
and sorrow and all the opposites
of this world,
until the final gasp when total night
descends on you,
and daytime will return
and ever return when you are gone forever,
for life must give life, not death.

I cherished the silences in my life
when I can think
and feel the texture and content
of my being
in the context of my world.
This silenced thought,
these silent incantations,
tell me where I've come from,
where I'm heading,
what I must redress, amend, restore
for the service I must render,
the reconnections I must make
among the living
and those alive in the
silence of eternal sleep.

When I can silence this chatterbox
I call my mind
a few minutes every day,
I taste the inner peace
in which there is no longer
any fear of death or danger,
nor sense of helplessness nor emptiness.
This is what the Hindu, Buddhist, African
elders teach me.

Silence is our call upon
the best in us
to fill us with the strength we need
to overcome
the demons of our being, those around us,
and the ghosts of our past,
and the nightmares of our
troubled selves,

to reaffirm the unity and harmony
we seek in humankind.

Silence is the workshop of my mind
where I'm making this poem.
For the truest poetry
comes from the untrumpeted
moments of life's unbroken melody,
heard and unheard.
Cuddle up in silence, my friend,
stretch out belly up
and breathe ever so silently,
and hear the body's juices flow:
There's more in that than what
these noisy know-alls
will ever let you hear and savour.

Of silence in our treachery
when we betray for power
or for money
or for blood lust
I cannot sing today: sorrow claws
at my vocal chords
while vultures blind the sun,
while the long unearthly cry
hangs over our smouldering land
and the dance of the demons can be heard all around,
while presidents and premiers
and entourage of sycophants
wave their flags from limousines and luxury trains
to assemble voting cattle.
That will be a dirge for yet another day:
for now let's listen to the music of
the Silent Hour, deep down
in the bowels of our being.

Nadine Gordimer
Look-alikes

It was scarcely worth noticing at first; an out-of-work lying under one of the rare indigenous shrubs cultivated by the Botany Department on the campus. Some of us remembered, afterwards, having passed him. And he – or another like him – was seen rummaging in the refuse bins behind the Student Union; one of us (a girl, of course) thrust out awkwardly to him a pitta she'd just bought for herself at the canteen, and she flushed with humiliation as he turned away mumbling. When there were more of them, the woman in charge of catering came out with a kitchen-hand in a blood-streaked apron to chase them off like a band of marauding monkeys.

We were accustomed to seeing them pan-handling in the streets of the city near the university and gathered in this vacant lot or that, clandestine with only one secret mission, to beg enough to buy another bottle; moving on as the druids' circle of their boxes and bits of board spread on the ground round the ashes of their trash fires was cleared for the erection of post-modern office blocks. We all knew the one who waved cars into empty parking bays. We'd all been confronted, as we crossed the road or waited at the traffic lights, idling in our minds as the engine of the jalopy idles, by the one who held up a piece of cardboard with a message running out of space at the edges: NO JOB IM HUNGRY EVEYONE HELP PLeas.

At first; yes, there were already a few of them about. They must have drifted in by the old, unfrequented entrance down near the tennis courts, where the security fence was not yet completed. And if they were not come upon, there were the signs: trampled spaces in the bushes, empty bottles, a single split shoe with a sole like a lolling tongue. No doubt they had been chased out by a patrolling security guard. No student, at that stage, would have bothered to report the harmless presence; those of us who had cars might have been more careful than usual to leave no sweaters or radios visible through the locked windows. We followed our familiar rabbit-runs from the lecture rooms and laboratories back, forth and around campus, between residences, libraries, Student Union and swimming pool, through avenues of posters making announcements of debates and sports events, discos and rap sessions, the meetings of Muslim, Christian or Jewish brotherhoods, gays or feminist sisterhoods, with the same lack of attention to all but the ones we'd put up ourselves.

It was summer when it all started. We spend a lot of time on the lawns around the pool, in summer. We swot down there, we get a good preview of each other more or less nude, boys and girls, there's plenty of what you might call foreplay – happy necking. And the water to cool off in. The serious competitive swimmers come early in the morning when nobody else is up, and it was they who discovered these people washing clothes in the pool. When the swimmers warned them off, they laughed and jeered. One left a dirt-stiff pair of pants that a swimmer balled and threw after him. There was argument among the swimmers; one felt the incident ought to be reported to Security, two were uncomfortable with the idea in view of the university's commitment to being available to the city community. They must have persuaded him that he would be exposed for elitism, because although the pool was referred to as The Wishee-Washee, among us, after that, there seemed to be no action taken.

Now you began to see them all over. Some greeted you smarmily (*my baas*, sir, according to their colour and culture), retreating humbly into the undergrowth, others, bold on wine or stoned on meths, sentimental on pot, or transformed in the wild hubris of all three, called out a claim (Hey man, *Ja boetie*) and even beckoned to you to join them where they had formed one of their circles, or huddled, just two, with the instinct for seclusion that only couples looking for a place to make love have, among us. The security fence down at the tennis courts was completed, reinforced with spikes and manned guard house, but somehow they got in. The guards with their Alsation dogs patrolled the campus at night but every day there were more shambling figures disappearing into the trees, more of those thick and battered faces looking up from the wells between buildings, more supine bodies contoured like sacks of grass-cuttings against the earth beneath the struts of the sports grandstands.

And they were no longer a silent presence. Their laughter and their quarrels broadcast over our student discussions, our tête-à-tête conversations and love-making, even our raucous fooling about. They had made a kind of encampment for themselves, there behind the sports fields where there was a stretch of ground whose use the university had not yet determined: it was for future expansion of some kind, and in the meantime equipment for maintenance of the campus was kept there – objects that might or might not be useful, an old tractor, barrels for indoor plants when the Vice-Chancellor requested a bower to decorate some hall for the reception of distinguished guests, and – of course – the compost heaps. The compost heaps were now being used as a repository for more than garden waste. If they had not been there with their odours of rot sharpened by the chemical agents for decay with which they were treated, the conclave living down there might have been sniffed out sooner. Perhaps they had calculated this in the secrets of living rough: perhaps they decided that the Alsations' noses would be bamboozled.

So we knew about them – everybody knew about them, students, faculty, administrative staff, Vice-Chancellor – and yet nobody knew about them. Not officially. Security was supposed to deal with trespassers as a routine duty; but although Security was able to find and escort beyond the gates one or two individuals too befuddled or not wily enough to keep out of the way, they came back or were replaced by others. There was some kind of accommodation they had worked out within the order of the campus, some plan of interstices they had that the university didn't have; like the hours at which security patrols could be expected, there must have been other certainties we students and our learned teachers had relied on so long we did not realize that they had become useless as those red bomb-shaped fire extinguishers which, when a fire leaps out in a room, are found to have evaporated their content while hanging on the wall.

We came to recognize some of the bolder characters; or rather it was that they got to recognize us – with their street-wise judgment they knew who could be approached. For a cigarette. Not money – you obviously don't ask students for what they themselves are always short of. They would point to a wrist and ask the time, as an opener. And they must have recognized something else, too; those among us who come to a university because it's the cover where you think you can be safe from surveillance and the expectations of others have of you – back to play-school days, only the sand-pit and the finger-painting is substituted for other games. The dropouts, just cruising along until the end of the academic year, sometimes joined the group down behind the grandstands, taking a turn with the zoll and maybe helping out with the donation of a bottle of wine now and then. Of course only we, their siblings, identified them; with their jeans bought ready-torn at the knees, and hair shaved up to a top-knot, they would not have been distinguished from the younger men in the group by a passing professor dismayed at the sight of the intrusion of the campus by hobos and loafers. (An interesting point, for the English Department, that in popular terminology the whites are known as hobos and the blacks as loafers.) If student solidarity with the underdog was expressed in the wearing of ragged clothes, then the invaders' claim to be within society was made through adoption of acceptable fashionable unconventions. (I thought of putting that in my next essay for Sociology II.) There were topknots and single ear-rings among the younger invaders, dreadlocks, and one had long tangled blond hair snaking about his dark-stubbled face. He could even have passed for a certain junior lecturer in the Department of Political Science.

So nobody said a word about these recruits from among the students, down there. Not even the Society of Christian Students, who campaigned for moral regeneration on the campus. In the meantime, 'the general situation had been brought to the notice' of

Administration. The implication was that they were to be requested to leave, with semantic evasion of the terms 'squatter' or 'eviction'. SUJUS (Students for Justice) held a meeting in protest against forced removal under any euphemism. ASOCS (Association of Conservative Students) sent a delegation to the Vice-Chancellor to demand that the campus be cleared of degenerates.

Then it was discovered that there were several women living among the men down there. The white woman was the familiar one who worked along the cars parked in the streets, trudging in thonged rubber sandals on swollen feet. The faces of the two black women were darkened by drink as white faces are reddened by it. The three women swaying together, keeping upright on the principle of a tripod. The Feminist Forum took them food, tampons, and condoms for their protection against pregnancy and AIDS, although it was difficult to judge which was still young enough to be a sex object in need of protection; they might be merely prematurely aged by the engorged tissues puffing up their faces and the exposure of their skin to all weathers, just as, in a reverse process, pampered females look younger than they are through the effect of potions and plastic surgery.

From ASOCS came the rumour that one of the group had made obscene advances to a girl student – although she denied this in tears, *she* had offered *him* her pitta, which he had refused, mumbling 'I don't eat rubbish'. The Vice-Chancellor was importuned by parents who objected to their sons' and daughters' exposure to undesirables, and by Hope For The Homeless who wanted to put up tents in this territory of the over-privileged. The City Health authorities were driven off the campus by SUJUS and The Feminist Forum while the Jewish Student Congress discussed getting the Medical School to open a clinic down at the grandstands, the Islamic Student Association took a collection for the group while declaring that the area of their occupation was out of bounds to female students wearing the *chador*, and the Students Buddhist Society distributed tracts on meditation among men and women quietly sleeping in the sun with their half-jacks, discreet in brown paper packets up to the screw-top, snug beside them as hot-water bottles.

These people could have been removed by the police, of course, on a charge of vagrancy or some such, but the Vice-Chancellor, the University Council and the Faculty Association had had too much experience of violence resulting from the presence of the police on campus to invite this again. The matter was referred back and forth. When we students returned after the Easter vacation, the blond man known by his head of hair, the toothless ones, the black woman who always called out *Hullo lovey how'you* and the neat queen who would buttonhole anyone to tell of his student days in Dublin, *You kids don't know what a real university is*, were still there. Like the stray cats students (girls again) stopped to scratch behind the ears.

And then something really happened. One afternoon I thought I saw Professor Jepson in a little huddle of four or five comfortably under a tree on their fruit-box seats. Someone who looked the image of him; one of the older men, having been around the campus some months now, was taking on some form of mimesis better suited to him than the kid-stuff garb the younger ones and the students aped from each other. Then I saw him again, and there was Dr Heimrath from Philosophy just in the act of taking a draw, next to him – if any social reject wanted a model for look-alike it would be from that Department. And I was not alone, either; the friend I was with that day saw what I did. We were the only ones who believed a student who said he had almost stepped on Bell, Senior Lecturer from Math, in the bushes with one of the three women; Bell's bald head shone a warning signal just in time. Others said they'd seen Kort wrangling with one of the men, there were always fights when the gatherings ran out of wine and went onto meths. Of course, Kort had every kind of pure alcohol available to him in his domain, the science laboratories; everyone saw him, again and again, down there, it was Kort, all right, no chance of simple resemblance, and the euphoria followed by aggression that a meths concoction produces markedly increased in the open-air coterie during the following weeks. The papers Math students handed in were not returned when they were due; Bell's secretary did not connect calls to his office, day after day, telling callers he had stepped out for a moment. Jepson, Professor Jepson who not only had an international reputation as a nuclear physicist, but also was revered by the student body as the one member of faculty who was always to be trusted to defend students' rights against authoritarianism, our old prof, everybody's enlightened grandfather – he walked down a corridor unbuttoned, stained, with dilated pupils that were unaware of the students who shrank back, silent, to make way.

There had been sniggers and jokes about the other faculty members, but nobody found anything to say over Professor Jepson; nothing, nothing at all. As if to smother any comment about him, rumours about others got wilder; or facts did. It was said that the Vice-Chancellor himself was seen down there, sitting round one of their trash fires; but it could have been that he was there to reason with the trespassers, to flatter them with the respect of placing himself in their company so that he could deal with the situation. Heimrath was supposed to have been with him, and Bester from Religious Studies with Franklin-Turner from English – but Franklin-Turner was hanging around there a lot, anyway, that snobbish closet drinker come out into the cold, no more fastidious ideas about race keeping him out of the mixed company, eh?

And it was no rumour that Professor Russo was going down there, now. Minerva Russo, of Classics, young, untouchable as one of those lovely creatures who can't be possessed by men, can be carried off only by a bull or penetrated only by the snowy penis-neck of a swan. We males all had understood, through her, what it means to feast with your eyes, but we never speculated about what we'd find under her clothes; further sexual awe, perhaps, a mother-of-pearl scaled tail. Russo was attracted. She sat down there and put their dirty bottle to her mouth and the black-rimmed fingernails of one of them fondled her neck. Russo heard their wheedling, brawling, booze-snagged voices calling and became a female along with the other unwashed three. We saw her scratching herself when she did still turn up – irregularly – to teach us Greek poetry. Did she share their body-lice too?

It was through her, perhaps, that real awareness of the people down there came. The revulsion and the pity; the old white woman with the suffering feet ganging up with the black ones when the men turned on the women in the paranoia of betrayal – by some mother, some string of wives or lovers half-drowned in the bottles of the past – and cursing her sisters when one of them took a last cigarette butt or hung on a man the white sister favoured; tended by the sisterhood or tending one of them when the horrors shook or a blow was received. The stink of the compost heaps they used drifted through the libraries with the reminder that higher functions might belong to us but we had to perform the lower ones just like the wretches who made us stop our noses. Shit wasn't a meaningless expletive, it was part of the hazards of the human condition. They were ugly, down there at the grandstands and under the bushes, barnacled and scaled with disease and rejection, no-one knows how you may pick it up, how it is transmitted, turning blacks grey and firing whites' faces in a furnace of exposure, taking away shame so that you beg, but leaving painful pride so that you can still rebuff, *I don't eat rubbish*, relying on violence because peace has to have shelter, but sticking together with those who threaten you because that is the only bond that's left. The shudder at it, and the freedom of it – to let go of assignments, assessments, tests of knowledge, hopes of tenure, the joy and misery of responsibility for lovers and children, money, debts. No goals and no failures. It was enviable and frightening to see them down there – Bester, Franklin-Turner, Heimrath and the others, Rosso pulling herself to rights to play the goddess when she caught sight of us but too bedraggled to bring it off. Jepson, our Jepson, all that we had to believe in of the Old Guard's world, passing and not recognizing us.

And then one day, they had simply disappeared. Gone. The groundsmen had swept away the broken bottles and discarded rags. The compost was doused with chemicals and spread on the campus's floral display. The Vice-Chancellor had never joined the bent backs round the zoll and the bottle down there and was in his panelled office. The lines caging Heimrath's mouth in silence did not release him to ask why students gazed at him. Minerva sat before us in her special way with matched pale narrow hands placed as if one were the reflection of the other, its fingertips raised against a mirror. Jepson's old bristly sow's ear sagged patiently towards the discourse of the seminar's show-off.

From under the bushes and behind the grandstands they had gone, or someone had found a way to get rid of them overnight. But they are always with us. Just somewhere else.

Acknowledgements

For permission to include copyright material in this book, the publisher is grateful to:

The author and Secker and Warburg for the extract from BOYHOOD (1997) by J M Coetzee; the author and Ravan Press for 'Athol Fugard and the New South Africa' from ATHOL FUGARD AND BARNEY SIMON: BARE STAGE, A FEW PROPS, GREAT THEATRE (1997) by Mary Benson; Nadine Gordimer for LOOK-ALIKES © Felix Licensing BV 1992; the author and Ravan Press for 'The Banquet' from THE KING OF HEARTS AND OTHER STORIES (1997) by Ahmed Essop; the author for 'Transfer' (first published in *Southern African Review of Books and Triquarterly*), 'Ground Wave' (first published in *New Contrast* and in *West Coast Line*) and *At the commission* by Ingrid de Kok.